The Blood Red Game

Also by Michael Moorcock
in Mayflower Books

The Blood Red Game

Michael Moorcock

Mayflower

Granada Publishing Limited
Published in 1974 by Mayflower Books Ltd
Frogmore, St Albans, Herts AL2 2NF

Originally published in Great Britain in
two parts in *Science Fiction Adventures* as
THE SUNDERED WORLDS and
THE BLOOD RED GAME
Copyright © Nova Publications 1962
Made and Printed in Great Britain by
Hazell Watson & Viney
Aylesbury, Bucks
Set in Linotype Times

For Barry Bayley

PROLOGUE

Renark was a wanderer in the galaxy for two years—but he was not lonely. Renark could never be lonely, for the galaxy was his omnipresent friend and he was aware of its movements. Even the peculiar control exercised on it by forces which he could not sense was as comforting as its presence. He moved about in it and contained awareness of every atom of it in his long, thin-boned skull. He wandered purposely through the teeming galaxy for two swift years and then, when ready, journeyed out towards the Rim . . .

ONE

The three of them met, at last, in a terrible town called Migaa on the harsh, bright edge of a wilderness. Both town and planet were called Migaa and it was the Last Chance planet for the galaxy's fugitives.

Renark disembarked from his cruiser, uncomfortable under the glare of the diamond-bright sun. He threaded his way through the great looming shapes of a hundred other ships, his mind searching the town ahead for his two friends. His skilled brain probed the shapes of streets and buildings, people and objects until at last he had located them, half a mile away on the other side of the town.

He strode briskly from the spaceport and there were no Customs officers to stop him here. He kept his friends' forms firmly fixed in his mind as he hurried in their direction. They were agitated and he guessed they might be in trouble.

People stared at him as he passed, a very tall, very gaunt man with deep-set black eyes in a long skull, a brooding face in repose. But they didn't stare at his face—they thought him remarkable mainly because he wore no apparent weapon. Almost all the men and women who came to Migaa came hurriedly—but they also came armed.

Only Renark walked purposefully along the metal-paved

streets, through the glinting steel buildings. The others moved aimlessly, wearing dark lenses to ward off the glare of the desert reflected in the steel and chrome of the buildings. He noted little transport on the streets, and what there was moved lazily. He thought the town had an exhausted air—yet at the same time it possessed an atmosphere of expectancy. It was a peculiar mood—and it smothered Migaa.

He noted also a shared quality in the faces of the men and women, a set expression which tried vainly to disguise the hope lurking in their eyes. They seemed afraid of hoping, yet evidently could do nothing else. Migaa—or what Migaa offered—was their last chance. It was Renark's too, but for other, less selfish, reasons.

When he reached the building where he sensed his two friends were, it wasn't the tavern he'd expected. This was called *The Drift Inn*, like hundreds of other taverns throughout the galaxy, but this one's name had a special significance.

He walked in to find tumult.

A fight was going on. He recognised several who could be either thieves or spacehands judging by the white, metal-studded plastileather overalls they wore. They were thick, brutal shouting men and they were attacking two others, not of their kind.

Renark recognised the pair. Paul Talfryn and young Asquiol of Pompeii, their backs against the far wall of the noisy, overcrowded public room. For a moment he felt the urge to leave them to it, confident that they would survive, but then he decided to help them. He wanted them to be as fit as possible for the forthcoming journey.

As he moved forward, a spacehand, using the whole of his metal-studded body as a weapon, launched himself at Renark. The spacehand had obviously learned his fighting techniques aboard ship or on a low-gravity planet. Migaa wasn't a low-grav world and the man's method of charging in an attempt to buffet Renark against the far wall didn't work. Renark skipped aside and the hand blundered past. Renark kicked against the base of the man's spine with a pointed boot. The spacehand collapsed backwards and Renark kicked him sharply in the head knocking him out.

Swiftly Renark pushed towards his friends.

Talfryn looked almost panic-stricken as he warded off the blows of his attackers, but Asquiol—flamboyant, grinning and vicious—was enjoying himself. A set of knuckle-spikes

6

gleamed on his right fist, and there was blood on them. One of Asquiol's opponents blundered back into Renark, clutching at a bleeding eye-socket.

'We're wasting time!' Renark shouted as the others saw him.

He moved into the crowd, pulling the tumbling spacemen aside with his large, ugly hands. Together, Talfryn and Asquiol punched their way towards him.

A growling giant swung a pocket-mace at Asquiol who ducked, crouched, then shot out his spike-covered fist deep into the spacehand's belly. The giant shrieked and the mace dropped from his hand as he fell to his knees.

The trio burst from the tavern and ran up a narrow side street until they saw the spacehands abandon the chase, shouting cat-calls from behind them. They turned into an alley, running between the backs of the buildings, their boots ringing on the metal.

'Which way to the Salvation Inn?' Renark said.

'Thanks for breaking that up,' Asquiol grinned. 'I thought you Guide Sensers could tell where anything was. It's this way. Not far.'

Renark didn't bother to use his space sensing ability. The image of what he had done to the spacehand was still sharp in his mind. He didn't like violence.

Asquiol led them back on to a main way. As they walked, Talfryn turned to Renark, his expression embarrassed.

'Sorry about that,' he said. 'Those hands were looking for trouble. They picked on Asquiol because of his clothes. We had to fight. We managed to avoid a dozen others, but couldn't get out of this one. The whole damned town's the same—tense, nervous, impatient.'

'I'm afraid I encouraged them,' Asquiol said. 'Really, one can't have one's dress insulted by such a vulgar breed!' He collapsed his knuckle-spikes and put them away.

Lonely and time-begrimed for all his youth, Asquiol dressed with careful flamboyance. He wore a high-collared, quilted jacket of orange ny-fur and tight slacks of purple stuff which fitted over his pointed, fibre-glass boots. His face was pale and tapering, his black hair cut short in a fringe over his forehead. He carried a slender, anti-neutron beamer —an outlawed weapon.

Asquiol had once been a prince—independent Overlord of

7

Pompeii, before the Galactic Lords enforced their powers and brought the planet into the Union.

Renark remembered that Asquiol had lost his title and estates for protecting him, and he was grateful.

He noticed that the younger man had lapsed into a brooding mood. It was his usual reaction and because of it many people thought him unbalanced, though Renark knew that Asquiol was the very opposite. His was a fine, delicate balance which only his will maintained.

Talfryn, lean-faced like his two friends, sensitive and bearded, was an unlicensed explorer and therefore a criminal. He was dressed conservatively—sleeveless jerkin of unstained hide, blue shirt and black trousers. He carried a heavy power-gun. He looked curiously at Renark, but since he said nothing Renark remained silent.

Then he smiled. His thin, grim lips quirked upwards and he straightened his back, turning his long head and looking hard at Talfryn.

Talfryn seemed disturbed by the look, and felt obliged to speak, so he said: 'When do we leave? I'm impatient to get started.'

Renark did not respond for a moment, and just kept looking.

Talfryn said: 'I can't wait.'

'I'm not sure yet,' Renark said.

As they reached the tall, many-windowed structure of the Salvation Inn, on the edge of town, Talfryn said to Renark: 'You told us we were wasting time back there. How much time have we, roughly?'

'Maximum, thirty-six hours,' the Guide Senser replied.

Asquiol looked up, startled out of his mood. He seemed troubled. 'Is that all?'

'That's all—probably less. I can feel it coming closer to this continuum all the time, but it's difficult to keep a fix on it always. It takes most of my energy.'

They entered the wide, high-roofed public hall of the Salvation Inn. Asquiol looked around him, seeking someone in the crowd, but was disappointed. The huge windows which stretched up one wall lighted several tiered galleries and looked out on to the bright black and white carbon desert of the planet.

They pushed through the crowd of men and women of many types. There were richly clad men; ragged men; men

8

who drank heavily and men who sipped at a single drink; vociferous men and quiet men. Here, as in the rest of the town, there was an air of tired, tense expectancy—an atmosphere which had lasted, this era, for thirty-seven years. All the residents glanced often at the big scanner screens suspended in the middle of the hall.

The screens would come to life only on particular occasions—when what they awaited entered the area of space on which they were always focused. When that happened —if it happened—there would be a rush for the spaceport and Migaa would be deserted again. Some people had been waiting in Migaa for over thirty years; others had died before their chance came.

The three climbed a narrow, winding stair until they reached a gallery occupied by a table and three chairs. They sat down.

'I had this reserved,' Asquiol said as he craned his neck to look down into the public hall.

Renark looked at him quizzically. 'I'm having the ship checked and re-checked,' he said. 'It's got to be ready very soon. The Shifter could materialise well before the maximum thirty-six hours I mentioned. Though it shouldn't be here for another twelve hours—judging by the rate it's been moving towards us since I contacted it twenty days ago.'

Renark paused, staring out across the terrible desert, screwing his eyes against the glare which penetrated even the polaroid windows.

'We've got to be ready,' he said. 'I can't tell how long it will remain in this continuum. There's also the possibility that it will go through the continuum at speed and we won't have a chance to get there before it travels on.'

'So we could have come to Migaa for nothing,' Talfryn shrugged. 'Well, my time's my own.'

'Mine isn't,' Renark said—but he didn't expand on that remark.

He was the only man in the entire galaxy capable of knowing when the Shifter System would materialise. Others who came to Migaa took the chance that the bizarre, continuum-travelling system would appear in the space-time during their own life, but it was a gamble. This was the only reason Migaa existed, built on the nearest halfway, habitable planet to where the Shifter would materialise. So

9

the outlawed and the damned, the searching and the hunted came to Migaa when there was nowhere else to go. And they waited.

Renark knew he did not need to wait, for he was a Guide Senser with a peculiar instinct, developed to the level of a science. He could locate, given only the vaguest direction and description, anything in the galaxy, whether it was a planet or a lost penny.

Needing no maps or co-ordinates, he could lead a person anywhere they wanted to go. He was a human direction-finder, and because of this he knew the Shifter was coming closer, for he had trained himself to see *past* his own space and out into other dimensions lying beyond, where there seemed to be hazy ghosts of planets—and suns almost, but not quite—like his own.

He had trained himself to see them, to prove a theory concerning the nature of the weird Shifter System which had been known to materialise—just suddenly *appear* in space and then vanish again without trace—only five times since mankind had reached the rim.

Little else was generally known about it.

The few explorers and scientists who had managed to reach the Shifter before it vanished again had not returned. It was impossible to say how long it would stay at any one time. The mystery system seemed to have a wildly erratic orbit, and Renark's theory that it moved on a course different from the rest of the universe—a kind of *sideways* movement—had been postulated years before when, as Warden of the Rim Worlds, he had been given the responsibility of sensing it—as he sensed the world and suns within his own continuum.

The time of the Shifter's stay varied between a few hours and a few days. It was never certain when it would appear or disappear. The desperate men who came to Migaa were optimists, hoping against hope that they would have the luck to be there when the Shifter arrived.

Though the Shifter received its title from Renark's own theory, it had several other names—Ghost System was a popular one—and certain religious-minded people ascribed some more dramatic significance to the system, declaiming that it had been cast from the universe for some sin its inhabitants had committed. These fanatics also had a name for the system—the Sundered Worlds.

10

And so a whole framework of myth had developed around the system, but very few dared investigate it for fear of being stranded. For the most part only criminals were willing to take the risk.

Renark stared down at the seething public hall. The Galactic Union's government machinery was near-perfect, its institutions difficult to abuse. This meant they could allow a greater degree of personal freedom for their citizens. But, because the government worked so well, criminals were hard put to escape the Union's laws. Migaa was their only hope. From Migaa they had the chance of escaping right out of the universe—unless the Galactic Police—the Geepees—made one of their sudden swoops on the town. For the most part the Geepees were content to leave well alone, but sometimes they hunted a criminal when he possessed some particular item or piece of information which they wanted. Then, if he eluded them long enough, they would come to Migaa looking for him.

Renark knew the Gee-lords sought him, that Lord Mordan, Captain in Chief of the Galactic Police, had his men scouring the galaxy for him. He wondered how long it would be before Mordan thought of Migaa.

Asquiol put his head in his hands and stared at Renark. 'Isn't it time we had your reasons for this trip, Renark?' He turned his head and searched among the crowd below. 'What made you quit your position as Rim Warden? Why wouldn't you tell the Gee-lords what you learned from that strange spaceship which landed on Golund three years ago? And why the passion to visit the Shifter?'

'I don't want to answer yet,' Renark told him. 'In fairness I should, but if I did it would give rise to further questions I can't possibly answer yet. All I can tell you right now is what you've guessed—I've been waiting three years to get to the Shifter, ever since I learned something of great importance from the crew of that spaceship on Golund. What they told me indirectly caused me to resign as Warden. As for the answers I don't have—I hope the Shifter will give me them.'

'We're your friends, Renark.' Talryn said, 'and we're willing to go with you for that reason alone. But if you don't find the answers you want out there, will you answer the original questions?'

'There'll be nothing to lose if I do,' Renark agreed. 'But

11

if you decide you don't want to come, then say so now. It's dangerous, we know that much. We might perish before we even reach the Shifter, and once there we may never be able to return.'

Both men moved uncomfortably but said nothing.

Renark continued: 'I owe you both debts of friendship. You, Paul, helped me in my research on variable time flows and were responsible for finally crystallizing my theory. Asquiol saved me from the attentions of that police patrol on Pompeii, sheltered me for six months and, when the Gee-lords found out, was forced, under the terms of his agreement, to give up his birthright. You have both made big sacrifices on my behalf.'

'I'm curious enough, anyway, to explore the Ghost System,' smiled Talfryn, 'and Asquiol has nothing to keep him here unless it's his new-found attraction for Willow Kovacs.'

Willow owned the Salvation Inn. She was reputed to be beautiful.

Asquiol appeared displeased, but he only shrugged and smiled faintly. 'You're right, Talfryn—if tactless. But don't worry, I'll still go when the time comes.'

'Good.' said Renark.

A woman came up the narrow stair leading to the gallery.

She moved in full knowledge of her slim beauty and her lips were curved in a soft smile. She was wearing the spoils of her conquests—her emerald-coloured dress was covered with jewels mined on a thousand planets. They flashed brightly, challenging the very brilliance of the desert. Her hands, heavy with rings, held a tray of hot food.

As she reached the table, Asquiol looked up at her and took the tray, making sure he touched her hands as he did so.

'Thanks,' she said. 'And hello—you must be the famous Warden Renark."

'Ex-Warden,' he said. 'And you're the young woman who has so disturbed our proud friend here.'

She didn't reply to that.

'Eat well, gentlemen,' she said, then returned down the staircase. 'We'll meet later, Asquiol,' she called over her shoulder as she made her way across the crowded floor of the great tavern.

Renark felt slightly troubled by this new intrusion. He hadn't been prepared for it. Although his loyalty to both his friends was great, he wanted Asquiol on the trip much more than he wanted Talfryn.

Asquiol was young, reckless, inclined to vindictive acts of cruelty at times; he was arrogant and selfish and yet he had a core of integrated strength which was hard to equate with his outward appearance.

But a woman. A woman could either complement that strength or destroy it. And Renark wasn't sure about Willow Kovacs.

Philosophically, and for the moment, Renark accepted the situation and turned his mind to the problem in hand.

'I think we should give the ship another check,' he suggested when they had eaten. 'Shall we go out to the pads now?'

Talfryn agreed, but Asquiol said: 'I'll stay here. I'll either join you out there or see you when you return. How long will you be?'

'I've no idea,' Renark said, rising. 'But stay here so that we can contact you if necessary.'

Asquiol nodded. 'Don't worry—I wasn't thinking of leaving the inn.'

Renark restrained an urge to tell Asquiol to be wary, but the Guide Senser respected his friend—it was up to the Prince of Pompeii to conduct his own affairs without advice.

Renark and Talfryn walked down the stairs, pushed their way through the throng and made for the door.

Outside there was a buzz of excited conversation. The two men caught some of it as they walked along the metal-paved streets.

'It seems there's a rumour that the Geepees are on their way in,' Talfryn said worriedly.

Renark's face was grim. 'Let's hope they don't get here before the Shifter.'

Talfryn glanced at him. 'Are they after you?'

'They've been after me for three years. Oh, it's not for any crime. But the Gee-lords came to the conclusion that I might know something of use to them and have been trying to get hold of me.'

'And do you know something of use to them?'

'I know something,' Renark nodded, 'but it's in their interest and mine that they don't find out about it.'

'That's part of your secret?'

'Part of the secret,' Renark agreed. 'Don't worry—if we reach the Shifter, I'll let you know it, for better or worse.'

He let his mind reach out into the void beyond the Rim. It was out there, coming closer. He could sense it. His mind trembled. He felt physically sick.

It was so wrong—*wrong*!

Implaccably, the impossible system was shifting in. Would it stay long enough for them to get to it? And could they reach it? If only he knew a little more about it. It was a big gamble he was taking and there was just a slim chance of it paying off.

Only he knew what was at stake. That knowledge was a burden he had had to strengthen himself to bear. Most men could not have done so.

As he walked along, glancing at the wretches who had so hopefully come to Migaa, he wondered if it was worth the attempt after all. But he shrugged to himself. You had to accept that it was worth it, he told himself.

There were none there who might have been properly described as extra-terrestials. One of the discoveries Man had made when settling the galaxy was that he represented the only highly-developed, intelligent life-form. There were other types of animal life, but Earth, throughout the galaxy, had been the only planet to bear a beast that could reason and invent. This was an accepted thing amongst most people, but philosophers still wondered and marvelled and there were many theories to explain the fact.

Two years previously Renark had suddenly resigned from his position as Warden of the Rim Worlds. It had been an important position and his resignation had given rise to speculation and gossip. The visit of an alien spaceship, supposedly an intergalactic craft, had not been admitted by the Galactic Lords. When pressed for information they had replied ambiguously. Only Renark had seen the aliens, spent much time with them.

He had given no explanation to the Gee-lords and even now they still sought him out, trying to persuade him to take over a job which he had done responsibly and imaginatively. Space-sensers were rare, rarer even than other psi-talents—and a Guide Senser of Renark's stature was that much rarer. There were only a few G.S. men in the entire galaxy and their talents were in demand. For the most part they acted as pilots and guides on difficult runs through hyperspace, keeping, as it were, an anchor to the mainland and giving ships exact directions how, where and when to enter normal space. They were also employed on mapping the galaxy and any changes which occurred in it. They were invaluable to a complicated, galaxy-travelling civilisation.

So the Gee-lords had begged Renark to remain Warden of the Rim even if he would not tell them who the visitors to Golund had been. But he had refused, and two years had been spent in collecting a special knowledge of what little information was known about the Shifter. In the end they had resorted to sending the Geepees after him, but with the help of Talfryn and Asquiol he had so far evaded them. He prayed they wouldn't come to Migaa before the Shifter materialised.

Renark had fitted his ship with the best equipment and instruments available.

This equipment, in his eyes, included the dynamic, if erratic, Asquiol and the easy-going Paul Talfryn. Both had helped him in the past because they admired him. He, in turn, responded to the sense of loyalty for them that he felt—and knew he could work best with these two men.

Several hundred ships were clustered in the spaceport. Many had been there for years, but all of them were kept in constant readiness for the time when the Shifter might be sighted.

Certain ships had been there for a century or more, their original owners having died, disappointed and frustrated, never having achieved their goal.

Renark's great spacer was a converted Police Cruiser which he had bought cheaply—and illegally—rebuilt and re-equipped. It could be ready for take-off in half a minute. It was also heavily armed. It was against the law to own a police ship and also to own an armed private vessel. The Union owned and leased all commercial craft.

The spacer required no crew. It was fully automatic and had room for thirty passengers. Already, since landing, Renark had been pestered by people offering huge sums to guarantee them passage to the Shifter, but he had refused. Renark had little sympathy for most of those who gathered in Migaa. They would have received more mercy from the enlightened Legal Code, of which the Union was justly proud, than from Renark of the Rim.

Although Migaa itself was thick with criminals of all

15

kinds, there were few in relation to the huge human population of the galaxy. For nearly two centuries the galaxy had been completely at peace, although the price of peace had, in the past, been a rigid and authoritarian rule which had, in the last century, thawed into the liberal government which now had been elected to serve the galaxy.

Renark had no hatred for the Union which pestered him. He had served it loyally until he had acquired that certain knowledge which he had withheld from the Galactic Lords. They had asked many times for the information he possessed, but he had refused; and he was cautious, also, never to let his whereabouts be known.

He glanced up into the blazing white sky as if expecting to see a Geepee patrol falling down upon them.

Slowly, the two men walked across the pad towards the cruiser.

Mechanics were at work on Renark's ship. They had long since completed their initial check and found the ship completely spaceworthy. But Renark had not been satisfied. Now they checked again. Renark and Talfryn entered the elevator and it took them into the centre of the ship, to the control cabin.

Talfryn looked admiringly around the well-equipped cabin. He had the scientist's eye that could appreciate the ingenuity, the skill, the energy, the pure passion which had gone into its construction.

Once, a year before, Renark had said in a talkative moment: 'Take note of these instruments, Talfryn—they represent man's salvation. They represent the power of the mind to supercede the limitations of its environment, the power of every individual man to control, for the first time, his own destiny.'

Renark hadn't been referring to his own particular instruments and Talfryn knew that.

Now, Talfryn thought, the mystique attached to science had made it at once a monster and a salvation. People believed it capable of anything, because they had no idea any more what it was. And they tended to think the worst of it.

More men like Renark were needed—men who could not take the simple workings of a turbine for granted, yet, at the same time, could take the whole realm of science for granted.

Just then another thought occurred to Talfryn—a thought

16

more immediately applicable to their present situation. He said:

'How do we know that our drive—or any of our other instruments—will work in the Shifter, Renark?' He paused, looking around him at the tall, heaped banks of instruments. 'If, as you think might be possible, different laws of space and time apply, then we may find ourselves completely stranded in the Shifter's area of space—cut adrift without control over the ship.'

'I admit we don't know whether our instruments will work out there,' Renark agreed, 'but I'm prepared to risk the fact that we may share certain laws with the Shifter. Maybe I'll be able to tell when it's closer, but my judgment won't be infallible.'

As a space senser, Renark needed no equipment to heighten his powers, but he did need to concentrate, and he therefore used an energy-charger, a machine which replaced natural, nervous and mental energy as it was expended and could, if used wisely, give a man an extra boost if he needed it especially. It was equipment normally only issued to hospitals.

Now, as Talfryn studied the recordings which had been made of the Shifter and became increasingly puzzled, Renark got into a comfortably padded chair and attached electrodes to his forehead, his chest and other parts of his body. He held a stylus and a plastic writing block on the small ledge in front of him.

Calmly, he switched on the machine.

TWO

Renark concentrated.

He could feel the presence of the galaxy, spreading inwards from his own point in space; layer upon layer of it, time upon time.

He was aware of the galaxy as a whole and at the same time felt the presence of each individual atom in its structure—each atom, each planet, each star, nova and nebula. Thorough space, where matter was of minimum density, little cores of denser matter moved. Spaceships.

17

Faintly, beyond the limits of his own galaxy, he sensed the lesser density of intergalactic space, and beyond that he picked up faraway impressions of other galaxies.

There was nothing unpleasant happening out there— something he already knew about. Something he was pledged to alter.

Then he adjusted his mind so that, instead of sensing the components of the galaxy, he sensed it as a whole. He widened his reception to take in a small area beyond the galaxy and immediately the entire structure of time and space, as he knew it, was flawed.

There was something there that was alien—something that did not fit. It was as if a body had moved through that small area and had torn a hole in the very fabric of the universe. His mind and body trembled as he sought to adjust, as previously, to his new, unnatural factor. It was a binary star with eleven planets equidistantly encircling it.

It did not exist. Not in relation to the universe Renark knew. He could make no close assessment of its components —as yet. It was wrong! Renark controlled his mind against the thought and concentrated on judging the system's progress. It was, in relation to itself, travelling through space in the same manner as ordinary stars and planets travelled. But it also travelled through a series of dimensions of which Renark had no experience whatsoever. And its course, its orbits through the dimensions was bringing it closer to Renark's own continuum.

He opened his eyes, gasping.

Quickly, he jotted down an equation; closed his eyes and re-adjusted his mind.

It continued towards them. It shifted through myriad alien dimensions, moving through a whole series of continua, progressing imperturbably onwards in an orbit as constant as the orbits of its planets about its stars. Soon now it would be passing through Renark's continua.

But how long would it stay there? Renark could not tell without knowing a little of the universes which lay beyond his own—and of these he had much to find out. His future plans depended on it.

In less than twenty minutes, Renark was finished. He looked over Talfryn's shoulder at the records.

'She's coming closer,' he said. 'Between twelve to fifteen hours and she'll be here. That's if my calculations are right.

I think they are. As far as I can tell, she's travelling at a regular rate. I can't explain why the periods spent in this continuum have varied so much, though, if her speed is as constant as it seems to be.'

'Well, you've narrowed it, anyway.' Talfryn's body seemed to tense.

'Yes.' Renark moved about the control room reading gauges.

'And you're certain it won't miss this space-time altogether?'

'That's possible—but unlikely.'

Renark stared at a bank of gauges for a moment and then he moved towards a chrome and velvet chair which had a whole bank of levers and switches in front of it, a laser-screen above it. This was the gunnery control panel.

Again he began to move uneasily about the great cabin. Again he volunteered a suggestion.

'We don't know all the directions in which our own universe moves,' he said. 'It may also, for all we know, have a "sideways" movement through the dimensions at an angle different from the Shifter. This would explain to some extent any inconsistency in the length of time the system stays in our space-time continuum.'

Talfryn shook his head. 'I've never been able to grasp any of those theories about the system. I don't even understand your ability to sense its approach. I know that, with training, space sensers can locate planets and even smaller bodies in normal space-time, but I wasn't aware that they could sense things outside, beyond, in different dimensions—wherever it is.'

'Normally they can't,' Renark said, 'but many who have probed the perimeter of space outside the galaxy have mentioned that they have sensed something else, something not in keeping with any recognised natural laws. Others have had the illusion of sensing suns and worlds within the galaxy—where suns and worlds just can't be! This has given rise to the theory of the "multi-verse", the multi-dimensional universe containing dozens of different universes, separated from each other by unknown dimensions . . .'

He paused. How could he explain in calm, logical words the sense of apartness, of alienness, he had received? How could he describe that shock, that experience which contradicted all he accepted with every sense he possessed, something that struck at the id, the ego, the emotions—everything?

He opened his mouth, trying to find words. But the words did not exist. The nearest way of expressing what he felt was to give vent to a shout of horror, agony—triumph. He didn't feel inclined to try.

So he shut his mouth and continued to pace the cabin, running his ugly hand over the firing arm of the big anti-neutron gun which had never been used. It was a savage weapon and he hoped there would never be need to use it.

Nuclear weapons of any sort made him uncomfortable. His strange sixth sense was as aware of the disruption of atoms as it was of their presence in natural state. It was an experience close to agony to sense the disruptive blast of atomic weapons. The anti-neutron cannon, beaming particles of anti-matter, was an even more terrible experience for him.

Once, as a child, he had been close to the area of a multi-megaton bomb explosion and his whole mind had blanked out under the strain of the experience. It had taken doctors a year to pull him back to sanity. Now he was stronger, better co-ordinated—but it was still not pleasant to be in a space flight.

Also, he loathed violence, considering it was the easy way out and, like many easy ways out, not a way out at all but only continuation of a vicious circle. So whenever possible he avoided it.

However, he was prepared, in this case, to use it—if it meant using it against anything in the Shifter which attempted to stop him in his avowed objective.

Renark had geared himself to drive towards one aim, and one only. Already he was driving towards it and nothing—nobody—would stop him. He was dedicated, he was fanatical—but he was going to get results if that was possible. If it wasn't possible, then he'd die trying to make it possible.

Soon, now—very soon—the Shifter would enter their area of space. He was going there. The Shifter offered the only chance in the universe of supplying him with the information he needed.

He glanced back at Talfryn, who was still studying the records.

'Any clearer?' he asked.

Talfryn shook his head and grinned.

'I can just understand how the Shifter orbits through

dimensions hitherto unknown to us, in the same way as we orbit through time and space, but the implications are too big for me. I'm bewildered. I'm no physicist.'

'Neither am I,' Renark pointed out. 'If I were I might not be so affected by the Shifter. For instance, there's something peculiar about any system comprised of a G-type binary star and eleven planets all equidistant from it—something almost artificial. If it is artificial—how did it happen?'

'Maybe it's the other way about,' Talfryn suggested vaguely. 'Maybe the planets all being the same distance away from the parent suns has something to do with the peculiar nature of the system. If they are a natural freak, could this have caused the Shifter's orbit?'

Renark nodded. He thought for a moment before he said:

'If you take for granted that Time is cyclic in accordance with the other known laws of the universe—although, as you well know, my own experiments seem to prove that there is more than one particular time flow operating in our own universe —if you take that for granted, however, we can describe the rest by means of circles.'

He walked to the chair where he had left his stylus and pad, picked them up and moved over the chart table.

'The Shifter orbits this way'—he drew a circle—'whereas *we* progress this way.' He drew a half-circle cutting horizontally through the first circle.

'Imagine that we have a finite number of space-time continua each with some mutually shared laws.' He drew a number of other half-circles below and above the first. 'They're all, like us, travelling this way. There is no contact between us but we exist side by side without being aware of each other's presence, all revolving in different sets of dimensions.'

Talfryn nodded.

'Imagine that the normal continua, as we understand the word normal, are orbiting horizontally, as it were. Then imagine that the Shifter is orbiting *vertically*. Therefore, instead of going its way without ever touching other alternate universes, its course takes it *through* them.'

'But wouldn't it take millions of years to complete a cycle like that?'

'Not necessarily. We know it doesn't, because we can't use temporal and spatial values and apply them to something as different as the Shifter. It has rules of its own which seem erratic to us but are probably as ordered in relation to itself as ours are to us.'

'You've got to take quite a bit for granted,' Talfryn sighed.

'Our scientists have been doing extensive research into the "multiverse" theory. They're pretty convinced.'

'Life and the universe,' said Talfryn, seating himself in a chair, 'are getting too complicated.'

Renark laughed shortly. 'One thing's clear, Talfryn—there are going to be a lot of mysteries solved and a lot of new ones started when we reach the Shifter. No one has ever returned from it.'

He glanced up suddenly. A light was blinking on the control panel.

'That's the intercom,' he said. 'Might be Asquiol or one of the engineers. Could you deal with it, Paul?'

Talfryn walked over and picked up the instrument. He flipped a switch but no picture appeared on the screen. He listened briefly and then turned back to regard Renark.

'Asquiol's here—and he's brought that girl with him.'

'What?' Renark for a moment lost his equilibrium. 'Why?'

'That's the other thing—that's why they came here so fast. The Geepees have arrived—they're looking for you!'

Renark pursed his lips. He should have been ready for a police raid but he had been so busy explaining the Shifter to Talfryn that he hadn't been on the look out for them.

Asquiol and Willow Kovacs stepped out of the elevator.

Asquiol said nervously: 'Sorry about this, Renark—but these are my terms.'

Renark shrugged. 'Terms?' He leant over the control panel adjusting dials. 'What's happening out there?'

'The Geepees are scouring Migaa asking if you're there. I got out as fast as I could. They'd be likely to recognise me and connect me with you.'

'Good.'

'You're willing to have Willow along on the trip?'

'You've told her the risks?'

'Yes.'

Renark sighed. 'I thought this might happen—knowing you. But I want you with us—and even if she's included in your conditions, I'm willing to concede to them.'

Renark forced away his irritation. There was no room for petty emotions in his plans. Only he knew what hung on his reaching the Shifter and discovering its nature and its cause.

22

Matters of personalities could not be considered. Action, not argument, was required of him now.

He had to pray that the Geepees wouldn't discover him before the Shifter materialised. They'd have to sit tight and wait it out. With any luck the Geepees wouldn't make a search of the ships on the pads until after they had scoured the town.

Renark beamed a message to the engineers, telling them to clear away their equipment and leave the ship in readiness for take-off.

Then he sat in his chair and waited.

An hour passed.

Willow seemed uncomfortable, sitting there in her immaculate sheath dress, listening to the men talking and going over the equations Renark had made, the records of the Shifter, theories which had been put forward.

Renark said: 'Rumour has it that *this* planet has a large human colony. I think we should head for that—number eight by my reckoning. You can see I've marked it.'

He glanced at Willow, who appeared pensive—not used to being ignored, evidently.

She moved nervously on her seat, looking about her disinterestedly. Normally there seemed to be nothing that could break her usual self-contained attitude—an attitude that had been necessary in a town like Migaa. But here, for the first time, she was in the company of men even more self-contained than she was. And it obviously disquieted her.

At last Asquiol saw her discomfort and said half apologetically: 'Anything troubling you?'

She smiled without amusement, obviously piqued: 'A woman's place is in the galley,' she said. 'Where is it?'

If she had intended to throw Asquiol off balance she had not succeeded.

'You might as well,' he said. 'I guess I'll be quite busy from now on. I expect we'll want something to eat soon.' He pointed to a door, then bent again over the charts.

Shrugging, she left the control room.

'Willow had always been curious about the Ghost System, living as she had in its shadow all her life. But she had never seen it. For some reason it had allowed her to dominate all the many men in her life, for they had seemed to have a hunger which she could not satisfy—though they had sought in her that satisfaction and had, therefore, put themselves

23

in her power, thinking she had a secret she did not, in fact, possess.

Now she was going to the Shifter . . . on Asquiol's instigation. She was glad. These men, all three, offered her something she was unused to. A strength of character, perhaps, that she had never found in all the others who had come to Migaa.

Renark, Talfryn and particularly Asquiol offered her calm, controlled strength—a peculiar mixture of detachment and passion. She busied herself preparing the food, finding a well-stocked larder—for Renark enjoyed food.

Talfryn looked up from the charts, glanced at the scanner screen. He swore and moved towards the controls.

'Something's gone wrong with the laser. I'll try and . . .'

'Don't touch those controls!'

Renark's brain seemed to swell within his skull, excitement pulsing through him, his body pounding. He paused for a second, frowned, controlled himself and then said calmly:

'It's coming, Talfryn.'

He sent his mind out, probing. He felt the sudden presence of the alien system grow as it merged into his own space-time—a whole system plunging towards them out of the hazy twilight of the universe, rupturing time and space on its rogue orbit. Elation flooded through him as he ran towards the laser screen.

The other two stood close behind him.

He watched as visible lines of energy swept across the area of space where his calculations indicated the Shifter would appear.

Space seemed to peel back on itself as great, blossoming splashes of colour poured through as if from the broken sides of a vat, merging with the darkness of space and making it iridescent so that sections shone like brass and others like silver, gold or rubies, the whole thing changing, changing constantly, erupting, flickering, vanishing, re-appearing.

Then, faintly at first, as if through rolling, multi-coloured clouds, the Shifter itself began to materialise, growing clearer and clearer, coming into sharper focus.

And then it was hanging there, as solid as anything else in the universe, the clouds which had heralded its approach fading away. A new system had joined the galaxy.

But for how long, Renark wondered, would the eleven

planets hang, equidistant, around the blazing blue binary star?'

He rushed back to the control panel, pressed a single stud activating the ship's automatic circuits.

The ship lifted. It shrieked away from the spaceport, away from the Geepee vessels, and within minutes was in deep space straining towards the shifter.

Moving to a single-minded, prearranged pattern, Renark acted like a zombie, his eyes fixed on the weird system ahead, his body one with the streaking ship which leapt the space between the edge of the galaxy and the mystery worlds.

Willow came out, startled, saw the screen and began to tremble.

Asquiol looked at her, but she glanced away and hurried back to the galley.

Renark seated himself in the control chair, his arms outstretched over the complicated control board, checking every slight tendency for the ship to veer away from the Shifter.

At this distance the planets seemed, apart from their ordered positions around the suns, to be no different from any other system in the galaxy.

Yet they glowed like carefully set diamonds around the sapphire suns. The ship sped closer and Renark could observe the rotation of the planets around the twin star. They seemed to be moving very slowly. Yet the closer they came the faster the planets seemed to move.

The other two had taken their places. The ship's drive, buried in the core of the ship, could be heard now, humming with the strain.

Renark shouted: 'Talfryn, keep all communication equipment on *Receive*. Asquiol, don't use those guns at random—wait until I order you to, if it's necessary.'

He turned in his seat for a moment, stared at Asquiol. 'And don't, on any account, use the anti-neutron cannon.'

Asquiol grimaced.

Talfryn flipped switches.

Willow reappeared, bewildered by the suddenness of events. She was frustrated, wanting something to do. The men worked, with concentration and efficiency, to their prearranged plan. Again Asquiol was oblivious of her presence.

The planets came closer. There was something peculiar about several of them, particularly one at nadir-south-east of the binary.

As the Shifter got larger on the screen, the communications panel began to squeal and moan.

'We're picking up its static, anyway,' Talfryn commented.

'They must be panicking on Migaa,' Asquiol grinned. 'The quicker we move the less chance we've got of getting caught up with the mob when they come out.'

'They'll be fighting the Geepees right now,' Renark said. 'They won't even let a fleet of battle-wagons stop them reaching the Shifter after waiting so long.'

'That'll delay both sides for a while,' Asquiol said.

'Let's hope the delay will be a long one.' Renark stared at his screen. 'What's ahead of us to starboard, Talfryn? Looks like a small fleet of some sort.'

Talfryn moved dials. 'You're right—spaceships of a kind I don't recognise. We'd better head for the nearest planet and try to escape them. The way they're coming up, they don't look friendly.'

The twin star was very close and bright now, blacking out the planets on Renark's laser screen.

Asquiol broke the energy seals on the guns with the key Renark handed him.

About ten of the weird ships came jolting closer, the metal of their hulls giving off a peculiar, yellowish glint. They pulsed through space and there was something menacing in their approach. Then they veered away, describing a long curve, and began to circle the area through which Renark's cruiser would have to pass.

Then, with a jerk which seemed to tug at their nerves and muscles and threaten to turn their bodies inside out, they entered alien space. They were in the Shifter's territory now —that was why the other ships had come no further, but awaited them. Their senses blanked momentarily, they felt dizzy, sick. Renark, feeling his senses going, sent out a desperate tendril of mental energy, anchoring himself to the Shifter ahead. Also he felt the presence of the darting alien ships. The metal of their construction was unfamiliar to him.

Then, suddenly, his whole mind seemed to explode as the fabric of space was ripped apart.

He gasped with the agony, forced his eyes open. He looked at the screen, and the planets, no longer whirling so rapidly around the binary, were moving at a more leisurely pace.

An inhuman growl rumbled through the control room. Talfryn worked the receiver, trying to pick up a picture, but couldn't. The growl came again but the language was un-recognisable. The leading vessel of the yellow fleet moved.

It seemed to turn over on itself, described a couple of somersaults, and then sent a coiling blast of energy before the humans' ship.

Renark blocked his mind and tensed his body. 'Screens!' he yelled.

But Asquiol had already raised them.

The ship shuddered and the screens proved effective against the alien weapons—but only just. Asquiol aimed the energy-laden guns on the leading ship.

'The anti-neutron cannon would dispose of them quickly enough,' he said wistfully.

'And probably the system as well,' Talfryn added as Asquiol's rapid shots bit into the alien ship, and it exploded to form, almost immediately, nothing more than a ball of ragged metal.

Now the other ships came on in formation. But Asquiol bent over his guns and grimly pressed his fingers down on all studs. The ship took the enemy retaliation, but shuddered horribly. His own fire damaged two, which then spiralled away from their comrades.

Then the whole fleet sailed up in the strange, somersaulting motion and fired together.

'We can't take this attack!' Talfryn screamed.

Asquiol's eyes were intent on the enemy craft. He sent another great blast of energy slamming through space as the force of the joint attack hit the cruiser.

The ship shook, shuddered, groaned and came to a dead stop. Lazily it began to spiral through space while more of the alien ships came flooding up from the nearest planet. Asquiol did what he could to stop them, but with the ship out of control it was difficult to aim.

Renark was fighting the controls.

'We took it,' he shouted, 'but it's thrown our circuits crazy. Talfryn, get down there and see what you can do with the Master Co-ordinator!'

Talfryn scuttled from his seat and entered the elevator, dragging a space suit with him.

Asquiol, eyes narrowed, aimed his guns carefully, cursing.

He cut down several more, but these ships didn't seem to care whether they were destroyed or not. Momentarily Asquiol wondered if they had living crews aboard.

Something was wrong with the quality of the void. It did not have its normal sharpness. Rivers of colour, very faint, seemed to run through, and shapes seemed to move just beyond the limit of his vision. It was tantalising, it was maddening . . .

Willow, pale and tense, clung to a bulkhead, her eyes fixed on the big laser screen. Space was alive with boiling energy. It swirled and coiled and lashed through the disturbed vacuum. To her, it was as if the binary had suddenly gone nova, for she could not see through the multi-coloured patterns of force which obscured everything but the yellow, darting shapes of the enemy ships.

Slowly the patterns faded, but the alien vessels came on.

Renark realised that the hideous nature of the void was not created by the force released in the battle. It was something else. Something much more ominous.

Asquiol kept up a rapid continuous fire. The screens took the brunt of the energy, but suddenly the ship was agonisingly hot.

Renark spoke into his mike.

'Talfryn, are you down there now?'

Talfryn's worried voice groaned back to him. 'I'm doing what I can. With any luck I should have fixed up most of the masters in five minutes.'

'Do it sooner,' Renark ordered, 'or you'll be dead.'

What were these aliens? Why were they so savagely attacking a ship when they hadn't even bothered to discover whether it was friend or enemy?

They came on with implacable ferocity.

Asquiol's lean face ran with sweat. Willow was on the floor now, her eyes wide, still fixed on the screens.

'Get into a suit, Willow,' he shouted. 'Get into a suit!'

She staggered up and walked unsteadily towards the locker from which she had seen Talfryn take a suit. Slowly she opened it, hissing with pain as the metal burned her hand, struggled to release a suit and clamber into it, its fabric automatically adjusting to the shape of her body.

Renark pulled on heavy gauntlets. The controls were now too hot for him to manipulate with bare hands.

Again and again the alien craft somersaulted and sent charges of energy towards the ship.

Asquiol felt his skin blister as he returned the fire and had

28

the satisfaction of seeing another three alien ships collapse into scrap.

Then Renark felt the ship responding again to the controls. Talfryn had fixed the Master Co-ordinator. He sent the ship veering away from the alien vessels.

Talfryn came rushing from the elevator, tearing off his helmet. He flung himself into his seat.

'Christ!' he shouted. 'More of them!'

Another fleet, larger than the one that had already attacked them, was coursing in to join the fight. As it got nearer, Talfryn noticed that the ships were not of the same design as the first fleet. In fact not one of these ships was of identical design. The weirdly assorted fleet fanned out—to engage not their ship but the enemy fleet!

Pale rays landed out and twined around the enemy craft, which vanished.

'By God, they're on our side!' Asquiol cried joyously as Renark eased his ship away from the area of the fight.

Suddenly a clear voice came over the speakers. It began giving directions. Talfryn moved the dials. 'I can't find the source,' he said. The voice, speaking their own language, although a slightly archaic version, began to repeat the directions in exactly the same tone as before—velocity, trajectory and so forth.

The ship was beginning to cool. The people inside relaxed somewhat.

'Don't bother finding the source,' Renark said. 'It sounds like a recording, anyway—an automatic instruction to visitors. We'll do as it says.'

Following the directions they found themselves shooting towards an ochre planet—small, ominous. The ships which had aided them now surrounded them, a motley assortment, but fast enough to stay with Renark's speedy cruiser.

When they were on course, a new voice broke into the taped instruction recital.

'Welcome to Entropium. We saw that you were in trouble and sent help. Forgive us for not doing so earlier, but you were then beyond our boundaries. You put up a pretty good fight.'

'Thanks,' Asquiol said softly, 'but we could have done with that help sooner.' Except in rare instances, Asquiol was not a grateful young man.

'That was out of the question,' the voice said lightly. 'But you're all right now, barring accidents . . .'

They sped down into the glowing red shroud of the planet.

'. . . *barring accidents* . . .'

Again and again they went through the same action, unable to do anything, trapped into it, as if they were on a piece of film being run many times through a projector.

Every time they appeared to reach the planet's surface they found themselves heading through the red mist again.

Then they were in the mist and motionless, the voice speaking amusedly:

'Don't worry, this will probably last a short while.'

Exhausted as he was, Renark had to use his special space sense to get some kind of grip on the situation. But it was virtually impossible. One moment he felt the presence of the red planet, the next it was gone and there was nothing in its place.

Several times they repeated their action of dropping down towards the surface until, quite suddenly, they were flashing through the fog and emerged into daylight—pinkish daylight —observing the jagged face of a sombre-coloured planet which, in its wild texture, was like a surrealist landscape painted by an insane and degenerate artist.

Willow lay on the floor in her space suit, her eyes closed, and even the men fought to control their minds and emotions as they jarred and shuddered at the sight of the alien planet. It was unlike any other they had ever seen, unlike any planet in the galaxy they knew.

Why?

It wasn't simply the quality of the light, the texture of the surface. It was something that made them uncomfortable in their bones and their brain.

It seemed unsafe, insecure, as if about to collapse beneath them, to break up like a rotten melon.

'Follow the scarlet vessel,' said the voice on the intercom.

Then Asquiol, Willow and Talfryn had vanished and only Renark was in the ship moving down once again into the red fog of the planet.

Where were they?

Desperately he quested around him with his mind, but the madness of disordered space and time was all about him—a whirlpool of *wrongness*.

Talfryn reappeared.

Renark said: 'Where were you—what happened?' Then Willow reappeared, and Asquiol reappeared.

And suddenly they were back over the surface of the planet again.

'Follow that scarlet vessel,' the voice instructed.

This time they noted a sardonic quality. Asquiol smiled, sensing that out there was a fellow spirit, as malicious as himself.

Willow had been seriously affected by the phenomenon, particularly when she had found herself momentarily alone in the ship. How many ships had there been in those few moments.

The scarlet vessel was at the point of the phalanx of slim, round, squat or square spaceships surrounding them. It broke away from the main fleet and headed across the planet in a south-westerly direction. Renark turned his own ship after it. The scarlet vessel slowed and Renark adjusted his speed. There was a break and for a few seconds the ship travelled backwards then lurched and was moving forwards again after the scarlet ship. Ahead of them now they could make out the towers of a city.

The whole situation was taking on the aspect of a confused nightmare. Whether it was illusion or some physical distortion of reality, Renark simply couldn't tell.

Even the outline of the city ahead did not remain constant but wavered and changed.

Perhaps, Renark guessed, these hallucinations or whatever they were, were the effect of adjusting to the different laws which applied to the Shifter system. Their senses had been thrown out of gear by the change and were having to adapt.

He hoped, for the sake of his mission, that he *could* adapt.

'Entropium,' said the voice on the laser.

The scarlet craft arched upwards until it was vertical over the planet, and began to shudder downwards on an invisible repulsion field. Renark followed its example.

Cautiously, he nursed the ship towards the ground, still not sure that the planet would not suddenly disappear from around them and they would be once again in the thick of battle with the alien ships. The experiences of the past half-hour had shattered his nerves, almost sapped his confidence.

They landed on a mile-square field which was bare but for a collection of small buildings at its far end.

'What now?' Willow said.

'We disembark—we got here comparatively safely and we were aided. They'd be unlikely to go to all the trouble they did if they wished us harm. Also I'm curious to find out about the people of "Entropium".' Renark pushed his big frame into a space suit and the others followed his example.

'What happened back there?' Talfryn said a trifle shakily.

'I should imagine we experienced some sort of spacetime slip. We know nothing of this system to speak of. We must be prepared for anything and everything—we can't even be certain that actions we make here will have the results and implications they would have in normal space-time. We could, for instance, walk forward and discover that we were one step backwards, could jump and find ourselves buried in rock. Be careful, though—I doubt if anything as drastic as that will happen here, particularly since human beings seem to inhabit the world and have built a city here. But we must go warily.'

THREE

The scarlet spacecraft was the only other ship on what was obviously a landing field. They wondered where the rest of the fleet had gone. As they cautiously disembarked, they saw that the crew of the scarlet ship were doing the same. Some of the figures were human.

And, for the first time, they were seeing alien and obviously intelligent life-forms.

Renark checked his wrist gauge. 'Looks as if we don't need suits,' he said, 'but it's just as well to be careful.'

He was tense as he walked across the charred ground towards the other group. He studied the aliens mingled with the human beings.

There were two sextupeds with four arms each and completely square heads containing a row of tiny eyes and beneath them a small mouth; several hopping creatures similar to kangaroos but obviously reptilian; a long-legged creature who towered over the others with a body proportionately smaller, a round body supporting long, swinging arm tentacles and a round head.

The leader of the six human beings was young, smiling, fair and dressed in a style which had been out of fashion in the galaxy for two hundred years—a loose blue shirt, baggy trousers tucked into green gaiters, and with mauve pumps on his feet. Over the shirt was a pleated coat fanning out from his waist and dropping to his calves. His weapons included an unfamiliar pistol and a rifle slung over his shoulder. He swaggered.

'Move high, you load,' he said in a peculiar accent. 'How strong goes galaxy—same?'

'It's changed,' replied Renark, recognising in the youth's archaic slang a patois once used by the old CMG—the Criminal Musician's Guild which, two hundred years before, had been composed of men outlawed because they refused to play the specific kinds of music deemed 'healthy' by the music censors.

But, two hundred years ago, the Shifter had been unheard of and Migaa not settled. Renark was curious. He could understand that two centuries hadn't passed as far as the young man was concerned, the flow of time being different here. Yet there was something wrong.

'You're after me, aren't you?' the young man said. 'I blew the long note around two-twenty W.W. Three. You?'

'This is now four hundred and fifty-nine years after World War Three on Earth,' Renark said. 'We use a new reckoning, though. How did you get here? Mankind had only just reached the Rim when you were around.'

'Accident, com. We were on the run—chased by Geepy ships—ran straight here. Found strange mixture, man—I inform you—and everyone from future. You're the farthest into the future I've met. Kol Manage is my name. Let's go.'

'Go where?'

'Entropium.' He pointed at the city. 'Come on, it's a long blow.'

The city could be seen about two miles away, scarring the skyline with a peculiar assortment of massive structures, some horribly ugly. But at least its outline now seemed firm and definite.

'Haven't you got ground transport?' Talfryn asked.

'Sometimes, com—not today. We scrap it all. Too square . . .'

'Why was that?'

'It palled, you know—we build something different sometime.'

Renark fumed inwardly. This casual attitude was aggravating when he needed clear, definite answers to the questions concerning him.

There was little time to lose. Now they were here he wanted to get started on his investigations. Yet the careless attitude of the Entropites threatened to slow him down, even though they didn't deliberately try to curtail him.

'Who runs the planet?' he asked Kol Manage as the group began to straggle towards the city.

'We all do. I guess you'd call Ragner Olesson boss. That's where we're going now—he wants to see you. He likes to see all newcomers.'

'Can't we get there faster? I'm in a hurry.'

'Well, stop hurrying, man—you've come to the end of the track. Ease up—there's nowhere to hurry to.'

'What do you mean?' Renark's tense mouth was grim.

'What do you think? You didn't like it there—you'll have to like it here. Simple.' And Kol Manage refused to answer any further questions.

They reached the suburbs of the city and were watched incuriously by some of the inhabitants, human and unhuman.

The population and the buildings comprised a disordered rabble which Renark found distasteful.

They walked through dirty streets which didn't seem to lead anywhere and it was nearly dark before they got to a square skyscraper, alive with light in its many windows.

The peculiar apathetic atmosphere of the city was as strong here as anywhere, but Renark hoped that at least some answers to his questions would be forthcoming. The atmosphere, he noted, was similar to Migaa's—only ten times worse.

The youth's companions dispersed but Manage led Renark and the others into the skyscraper and up a couple of flights of grubby stairs. They came to a door and Manage pushed it open.

The four people stayed uncertainly in the entrance to the big chamber, which was an untidy combination of control room and living quarters. Manage walked across it.

Two men looked up coolly at his approach. Both were middle-aged. One was rugged and handsome.

Renark glanced in distaste at the place. Computers and other equipment lined one wall of the room. The floor was littered with carpets of clashing designs, papers, clothing and various objects—a couple of rifles, a flower vase, cups, files and books. Tables, chairs and couches were placed here and there in apparent disorder. The two men sat on a long couch near the largest computer. A door behind them opened onto another room.

'Enter,' said the handsome man casually to the four. 'We watched you come in—you made the quickest start I've ever seen. The rest shouldn't be here for a little while yet.'

'They're probably having trouble with a police patrol,' Renark said, entering with a degree of caution.

'I'm Ragner Olesson,' said the big man. He looked hard at Renark, obviously seeing something unfamiliar in the Guide Senser's stern expression—perhaps, erroneously, sensing a rival to his leadership.

'Renark,' said the ex-warden, 'these are my friends.' He didn't introduce them.

'Well, Mister Renark, all you need to know is this. Don't try to change things here. We like it as it is. You can do what you want in Entropium, anything you want at all—but don't interfere with us.'

Renark frowned, feeling himself growing increasingly angry. This wasn't the reception he'd expected, and casualness and disorder of the kind he saw was annoying in his present frame of mind. His whole being was geared to one thing, one object.

He said 'Are you the boss of Entropium?'

'If you like. But I don't push anyone around as long as they keep to themselves any ideas they've got of taking over or changing things radically. Get it?'

'Now, listen,' said Renark. 'I'm looking for information, that's all. Maybe you can help me.'

The man laughed, then sneered. He got up and swaggered closer to Renark, seeming a trifle agitated, however, as if Renark's statement was unprecedented.

'What kind of information, mister? We've got plenty of space to move around here, so go and look for it somewhere else. I don't like being disturbed. If you try to make troubles you can get off the planet'—he smiled sardonically—'or get killed. Your choice.'

Controlling himself, Renark said calmly: 'So what's expected of us now?'

'Look, you do what you like—so long as you don't bother anyone. Right now you're bothering me.'

'Aren't you interested in why we're here? You helped us fight off the fleet that attacked us. Why did you do that?'

'You're here like everyone else who comes, because you

35

don't like it where you came from. Right? We sent our fleet to help you because the more of us there are and the more ships we've got, the less chance the Thron—it was their ships that attacked you—have of invading us. Simple.'

'I'm here,' said Renark impatiently, 'to discover the nature of this system—what makes it work. I'm not a criminal on the run and I'm not just a casual explorer. The very future of humanity may well hang on what I discover or fail to discover here. Is that clear?'

Olesson's companion got up. He was an intelligent looking man with a tired face. His whole attitude was one of weariness and boredom.

'I'm Klein—I used to be a scientist of sorts. You won't find out anything about the Shifter, my friend. There's no line of enquiry you can follow that leads anywhere. Every fact you uncover is a contradiction of anything you've learned previously.'

Renark's voice was savage. 'I'm going to force the truth out of this system, Mister Klein.'

His companions moved uncomfortably and Asquiol's slender right hand rested on the butt of his anti-neutron beamer. They were well aware that they were outnumbered here. They didn't feel Renark's anxiety and were therefore less ready to alienate their hosts.

But Klein smiled slightly, showing no annoyance.

'There have been many who've tried—and all failed. The concept is too alien for us to grasp, don't you understand? It isn't a question of your capacity for reasoning or anything else. Why not just accept the fact that you're safe from the cares of the universe—the multiverse. Find yourself a niche and settle down. You can be quite comfortable here—nobody expects anything of you.'

'There must be *some* questions you can answer to give me a clue, a starting point?'

'Harry,' Olesson said impatiently, 'forget these bums, will you? Let them do what they like so long as they stop worrying us. Let them make their "investigations". They won't get anywhere.'

'I'm easy,' Klein said to Renark, ignoring his companion. 'But there's not much I can tell you. What do you want to know?'

'For a start, tell me something about the Shifter as you know it from living on it.'

36

Klein shrugged and sighed. 'We pick up all kinds of intelligent life-forms as we travel. Usually fugitives, sometimes explorers. They've settled on planets—if you can call it settled—that suit them best. Once on a planet, only a fool leaves it.'

'Why?'

'Because if the planets are wild, then space outside is wilder. A trip outside the atmosphere sends anyone quite mad. Why do you think nobody leaves the planets? Only the Thron are insane enough already to do it. You've seen it at its best—when it's been calmer. That's why we had to wait so long before sending out help—not many people dare to risk travelling in space most of the time. It's usually worse near the perimeter, too. You were lucky to get help at all.'

'What's wrong with it?'

'Nobody knows—but most of the time space out there is filled with chaos. Things appear and disappear, time becomes meaningless, the mind breaks . . .'

'But it wasn't too bad most of the time while we were coming here.'

'Sure. The Thron had something to do with that, I guess. They seem to know a bit more about controlling whatever it is.'

'Then, if that's so, there must be some means of discovering the real nature of the Shifter.'

'No. I reckon the Thron have just been lucky.'

Klein stared with curiosity at Renark.

'What exactly do you want to know—and why?'

'That's my business.'

'You've got a bigger reason than mere curiosity. You said so. You tell me and maybe I'll decide to go on. If not, I don't want to bother. I want to see what you're leading up to.'

'You can tell us now, Renark, surely,' urged Talfryn.

The ex Warden sighed.

'All right. About two years ago I made contact with the crew of an intergalactic spaceship. Though it had come from another galaxy, it wasn't so very different from ours—and the crew was human. This in itself was astonishing. They had not knowledge of our history, just as we had none about theirs. They landed on Gouland, a backwater planet under my jurisdiction. I went out to meet them. We learned one another's language and we talked. One of the things they told me was that, in *their* galaxy, human beings were the only intelligent life-form.'

'Just like ours,' Klein nodded.

'And, I suspect, just like any other galaxy in our particular universe. Tell me, Klein, where do the aliens we've seen come from?'

'Different space-time-continua. Every STC seems to have only one dominant, intelligent life-form. I can't explain it.'

'It must mean something. That's what I suspected, anyway. A phenomenon natural to every STC universe. But what isn't happening, I hope, in every STC, is what is happening in our particular universe.'

'Happening?' Talfryn spoke.

'The visitors from the other galaxy came to warn us. Their news was so terrible that I had to keep it to myself. To have released it would have been to start galaxy-wide panic.'

'What the hell is happening?' Even Olesson became interested.

'The end of the universe,' Renark said.

'*What!*' Talfryn gasped.

'The end of the universe—so far as humanity's concerned, at any rate.'

'And the Gee-lords don't know?' Asquiol said. 'You didn't tell them—why?'

'Because I was counting on the Shifter to offer a clue that might save us.'

'Not just the end of a galaxy,' Klein said softly, 'but an entire universe. *Our* universe. How do you know, Renark?'

'The visitors gave me proof—my own space-sensing ability did the rest. I'm convinced. The universe has ceased to expand.'

'That's a problem?' Olesson said.

'Oh, yes—because, not only has it ceased expanding, it is now contracting. All matter is falling back to its source. All the galaxies are rapidly drawing together—and at a far greater speed than they expanded. And the speed increases as all matter is drawn back to the hub of our universe! Soon all the galaxies will exist as a single mote of matter in the vastness of space. Then even that mote may vanish, leaving —vacuum. So far this inward movement is restricted to the galaxies, but, soon, when they all come together, it will involve the stars, the planets—everything.'

'This is theory,' Klein spoke softly.

'Fact,' said Renark. 'My visitors' experiments are conclusive. They have tested the theory in their laboratories and found that when the matter has contracted as much as it can —and it forms a pellet of astounding density—it just disappears. They believe that when it reaches the final stage it enters other dimensions as a photon, possibly in some greater universe—the one encompassing the multiverse, itself, perhaps.'

'So it disappears—like the shifter?'

'That's right.'

'I still don't know why you came here,' Klein said. 'Because it's safe? We *are* safe, aren't we?'

'I came here,' said Renark, more calmly now, 'in the hope of discovering a means of travelling into another universe.'

'You think because the Shifter travels through the multiverse that you can find out how it works and build some kind of machine that will do the same—is that it?' Klein seemed interested, even enthusiastic.

'That's it. If I can discover the Shifter's secret, I may be able to return to our universe. As a Guide Senser I could probably find it—and warn them of what's happening and offer them a means of escaping into a universe which isn't undergoing this change.'

Olesson put in: 'Whatever happens, we're all right eh?'

Renark nodded. 'Yes. But that doesn't appeal much to me.'

The others didn't reply. Although horrified, they also seemed relieved.

Renark sensed this. 'You're still with me?' he said to his friends.

'We've nothing to lose,' Talfryn said uncomfortably.

'Nothing,' agreed Asquiol.

The equipment beside them squealed. Olesson moved ponderously towards it, tuned in the receiver, got sound and a picture. 'Yes.'

The face on the screen said: 'More visitors, Ragnar—a big load from Migaa are coming in now.'

'The usual routine,' said Olesson, shutting off the receiver.

FOUR

Renark and his companions watched the screens as the shoals of craft from Migaa entered the Shifter's area of space.

Then the Thron ships came slashing upwards from their planet —like sharks. There was an insane, inexplicable anger in their ferocity.

From other directions a large, motley force of Entropium warships helped the Migaan craft dispose of the outnumbered Thron vessels. The fight was much shorter than Renark's.

'They're just in time,' commented Olesson, watching the screen. 'The system's due to begin transition again pretty soon. Better wave your universe goodbye, Renark. You won't be seeing it again for some time if at all.' He grinned callously.

Ignoring the big man, Renark turned to his friends.

'We'll have to split up. There must be people here who aren't just criminals—people who've made some attempt to explore or analyse the system. They can help us. Move about the city—ask questions.'

There was a peculiar note in Klein's voice. 'Go to see Mary the Maze, Renark. I can't guarantee she'll help, but she'll serve as a warning to you. She was an anthropologist, I hear. She explored as much of the Shifter as she was able. But go and see where her curiosity got her, Renark.'

'Where is she?'

'I'm not sure—but everyone knows her on Northside. You'll find her soon enough if you ask.'

'Okay, I will.' He said to the others: 'You take other parts of the city. Don't ignore any piece of information, speculation or rumour—it could all be useful. We've got to work fast!'

'But fast,' sneered Olesson as they left.

Walking out of the untidy building, they saw the bright arrows of fire searing down on the landing-field two miles away. They split up.

Renark had chosen the worst possible time to look for anyone.

As he went from hotel to hotel, from bar to bar on the north side of Entropium, the men and women from Migaa began to pour exuberantly in.

They got drunk quickly and the whole city came alive and excited. Not only human beings celebrated the new 'shipment's' arrival. Aliens of many kinds joined in with their own forms of merry-making.

Once, a creature like a giant cross between a slug and a caterpillar addressed him in high-pitched Terran, but he ignored it and moved on, searching, asking questions, getting incoherent or facetious replies.

And then the nightmare really began.

Quite suddenly Renark felt nausea flood through him, felt his vision blur and sent out a mind-probe which took in the whole of the system and part of the galaxy beyond it. His mind just refused to accept some of the information it received—he couldn't take it in.

The galaxy seemed distant, and yet retained the same point in space in relation to the Shifter.

Then the whole planet seemed suddenly engulfed by a weird, greyish mist. The darkness gave way to it.

For an instant, Renark thought he saw the buildings of the city begin to fade again. He felt weightless and had to cling to the side of a house. The house seemed solid enough, but its components moved beneath his hands and his own body seemed diffused, lacking its normal density. As his mind swirled, he returned it to the comforting reality of the galaxy, as he habitually did in times of stress. But the galaxy was no longer real.

It seemed ghostly, he was losing touch with it. He very nearly panicked, but controlled himself desperately.

Then he understood what was happening.

They were leaving the galaxy—leaving the universe Renark loved, that he was prepared to die for. He had an unreasoning sense of betrayal—as if the galaxy were leaving him rather than the reverse. He breathed heavily. He felt like a drowning man and sought for something to grab—physically and mentally. But there was nothing. Nothing constant. Nothing that did not change as he sensed or saw it.

The grey city seemed to tilt at an angle and he even felt himself sliding. He staggered on down the crazily angled street, his hands before him as if to ward off the maddening horror of all nature gone wrong.

The only thing he could cling to was abstract—something that could become disastrous reality—his reason for coming here. So he fought to remember that.

The trans-dimensional shift had begun. That was obvious. Realisation had come to the newcomers in Entropium almost simultaneously. There were pockets of silence in a hundred taverns throughout the city.

Realisation had come to the newcomers in Entropium himself to keep moving. Movement was something—movement proved he still had some control over his body if not over the insane environment he had entered. But, as the realisation came, his legs slowed without his noticing. He had trained himself never to regret anything resulting from his conscious actions, but now he had to fight the emotion rising within him. The emotion came with the understanding that his chance of returning to his own universe before the Shifter's orbit brought it back again was low.

He could not afford to relax now until his mission was ended, could not afford to risk following up a wrong line of investigation, could not afford to think of anything but his ultimate reason for coming here.

The ground rose up like a tidal wave and as suddenly subsided again.

He pressed on. His intensity of thought was savage. He tore at his own mind, trying to force every extraneous thought, every piece of unnecessary information, out of it, to make himself into a calculating, acting machine with one object—to wrench the Shifter's secret from the chaotic turmoil of the trans-dimensional system.

He forgot the emotion momentarily engendered by the shift.

Light suddenly faded, bloomed again, faded. The buildings seemed to shimmer like a mirage, the very axis of the planet seeming to tilt once more, and Renark fell flat, clutching at ground which crawled beneath his hands.

He heard confused sounds of fright.

He looked up and, through the ghostly shapes that billowed ahead of him, saw the doorway of a tavern. He staggered up and moved towards it. Finally, he was inside, looking at the people there.

The newcomers were patently terrified, but the old residents seemed to be taking the planet's disordered behaviour with equanimity. They were evidently used to it. This must happen every time the system shifted into a new section of the multiverse.

Hoarsely, he said: 'Where do I find Mary the Maze?'

He repeated the question until a swarthy man looked up from his girl and his drink and said:

'Rupert House—two blocks that way.' He pointed with his thumb.

The planet was still doing crazy things. It still flickered with alternate night and day; the ground seemed alive, liquid, crawling. But Renark pushed on through the nightmare until he saw the sign saying Rupert House.

He opened a door that made his hand itch, and went inside.

'Mary the Maze?' he said thickly to the first man he saw. The man, sharp-faced, small, dressed in black, said: 'Who wants her?'

'Renark wants her—where is she?'

The man stayed silent. Renark grasped him.

'Where's Mary the Maze?'

'Let go—she's upstairs where she always is—room Red Seven.'

Renark, his head thumping, half blind with the strain which the Shifter's transition was putting on his mind and metabolism forced himself up several escalators and found the room he wanted.

He knocked.

Then he opened the door.

Mary the Maze was a horrible sight. Beautiful, blank— debased, in her mumbling insanity, to a travesty of ideal humanity.

Renark saw immediately that she had obviously been a highly intelligent woman. She was still physically beautiful, with a lean, clean face, large brown eyes, wide mouth, long black hair and full breasts. She had on only a dirty skirt and her fingers wandered across an intricate keyboard of the kind once used on the over-complicated 'sentiment' spaceships, popular a hundred years before, until scrapped for their tendency to have 'nervous breakdowns' in emergencies. But there was only a keyboard—it was not wired to anything.

Renark's savage mood faded as he came softly into the little room, looked at its walls of bare plaster, the pilot's couch ripped from some ship and evidently used as a bed by the mad woman.

'Mary?' he said to the muttering wreck. 'Mary?'

She stared at him and the look in her eyes repelled him.

'Adam? Ah, no. Come in, Castor, but leave Pollux outside. Or is it Ruben Kave, Hero of Space, come to visit me?' Her mouth broadened, the lips curving upwards. She made a vague, graceful gesture with her hand. 'Do sit down,' she said.

There was nowhere to sit. He remained standing, disturbed, nonplussed.

'I'm Renark,' he said. 'I want information. It's important —can you help me?'

'Help . . .?' The voice was at first detached. Her fingers moved constantly over the keyboard. 'Help . . .?' Her face twisted. Then she screamed.

'*Help!*'

He took a step forward.

The hands moved more swiftly, agitatedly over the board.

'*Help!*' She began to emit a kind of soft scream.

'Mary,' he said urgently. He could not touch the smooth shoulders. He leant over the drooling woman. 'It's all right. They say you've explored the Shifter—is that true?'

'True? What's true, what's false?'

'What was it like, Mary? What did this to you?'

A groan, masculine and desperate, came from the woman. She stood up and walked unsteadily towards the couch, lay down on it, gripping the sides.

'What's the Shifter, Mary? What is it?' His face felt tight, as tight as his rigidly controlled emotions.

'Chaos . . .' she mumbled, 'madness—super-sanity—warmth. Oh, warmth . . . But I couldn't take it, no human being could—there's no anchor, nothing to recognise, nothing to cling to. It's a whirlpool of possibilities crowding around you, tossing you in all directions, tearing at you. I'm falling, I'm flying, I'm expanding, I'm contracting, I'm singing, I'm dumb—my body's gone, I can't reach it!'

Her eyes stared. Suddenly she looked at him with some sort of intelligence.

'Renark you said your name was?'

'Yes.' He was steeling himself to do something he didn't want to do.

44

'I saw you once, perhaps—there. Here. There.' She dropped her head back and lay on the couch mumbling.

He sensed the chaos of the Shifter brawling about in the back of his mind. He thought he knew how it could have turned her mad—felt some sympathy with what she was talking about.

He turned all his attention to her, using his sensing ability to sort her out into her composite atoms, concentrated on her sensory nerves and her brain structure in an effort to get some clue to the effect which the Shifter had had on her.

But there was little physically wrong, although it was obvious that the quantity of adrenalin flooding her system was abnormally high and that this, perhaps, was the reason for her almost constant movement.

But her mind wasn't open to Renark. He was not a telepath and was almost glad at that moment that he couldn't see into her wrenched-apart mind. Neither was he telekinetic, but nontheless he hated even this form of intrusion as he studied her muscle responses, her nervous system, in an effort to find some clue how to pull her together long enough to get some answers to his questions.

He felt her move.

'Asquiol!' she said. 'Isn't that a name—something to do with you? Aren't you dead?'

How could she possibly know of Asquiol?

'Yes. Asquiol's the name of my friend. But I'm alive . . .'

He half cursed the introduction of this new element of mystery in an already difficult situation.

'What about Asquiol?'

But there was no response from the mad woman, who had now resumed her vacant staring at the ceiling.

He tried another tack.

'Mary—where did you go? What did you discover?'

'The ragged planet,' she muttered. 'I go there—went there —last—the lattice planet. Stay away.'

Now he wanted to shake the information out of her but he had to coax.

'Why?' he said more gently. 'Why, Mary?'

'Doesn't travel with the Shifter—not all of it, some of it— exist in other dimensions, travelling independently? The Hole is there—the dwellers lurk in the Hole. They know everything —they mean no harm, but they are dangerous. They know the truth, and the truth is too much!'

'What truth?'

'I forget—I couldn't hold it. They told it to me. It wasn't fair.' She stared at him again and once more intelligence was in her eyes. 'Don't believe in justice, Renark—don't for an instant take its existence for granted. It doesn't exist. You learn that in the *gaps*, you can make it—but it breaks down in the real universe. You find that in the *gaps*.'

'Gaps? What are they?' He wondered at the peculiar accent she put on the word.

'The ragged planet's *gaps*.' She sighed and fidgeted on the couch. 'That's where I finally forgot—where every theory, every scrap of information gathered on the other planets was meaningless. And I forgot—but it did me no good. I was curious . . . I'm not now, but I want rest, peace, and I can't have it. It goes on. They know, though—they know, and their hate has kept them sane . . .'

'Who are "they", Mary?'

'The Thron—the horrible Thron. And the Shaarn know, too, but they are weak—they couldn't help me. The beasts. Don't let them push you into the . . . untime . . . the unspace. Their weapons are cruel. They do not kill.'

'Thank you, Mary,' Renark said, at a loss to help her. 'I will go to Thron.'

She rose from the couch, screaming: 'I said not, spiral, magenta, irri-bird, night. Not, sight of droan—*not*: Oh, no . . .'

She began sobbing and Renark left the room.

He walked down the corridor, brooding, dissatisfied with the little he had learned, but with a definite plan of action now. He must go to Thron and discover the truth of Mary's statement.

Whatever happened,, the Thron would be of more help—assuming they could be encouraged to help—than the decadent inhabitants of Entropium, who refused to know anything. Though he could half sympathise with anyone who didn't wonder or question. The boiling chaos of the Shifter as it moved through the dimensions of the multiverse was enough to disturb anyone.

He walked out of the hotel and found, to his relief, that the planet seemed to have quietened down and was presumably in normal space again, but in an alien universe.

Ah he walked swiftly towards the building, he allowed his mind to put out tendrils and was relieved when he sensed, beyond the insane perimeter of the Shifter, the solid, ordered planets and suns of a wide, spiral galaxy like his own in general components, although here and there he came across organic and chemical formations which he did not recognise.

When he got back to the control room in the skyscraper, Klein said: 'Half the new Migaa-load are dead. As usual, they panicked and caused trouble while we were in transit, so we cleaned them up. The rest are settling down or running back to the launching pads . . . How did you get on with Mary?'

'She said that the Thron knew about the Shifter's nature— or that's what I believe she said.'

Asquiol and Willow, both pale, walked in. He nodded to them.

'Were the Thron the race who initially attacked us?' he asked Klein.

Far away he heard ships blasting off. Klein cursed. 'They were warned. That's another lot on their way to death.'

'What do you mean?'

'Every time there are newcomers who try to use the Shifter as a transport from their own universe to another, we warn them that once they're here they're stuck. But they try. Maybe one or two make it—I don't know. But I think not. Something stops you leaving the Shifter once you're here.'

'It's impossible to get off?' Willow said worriedly.

Renark glanced at Willow. It was funny, he thought, how crisis took different people in different ways. Willow sounded as if she was going to break down. Asquiol evidently hadn't noticed it. He was curious to see how Talfryn would look and act when he came back.

Klein was talking. 'That's right, honey. It's harder to get out than in. You don't exist *entirely* in the space-time matrix of the universe which the Shifter is currently in. We kind of overflow into other dimensions. So when you try to leave, you hit the dimensions at a slight angle and—*whoof!* you break apart. Some of you goes one way, some of you goes another. No, you can't get out.'

'Renark—you have more problems,' Asquiol said, fiddling with his gloves.

'And more coming, from what I've learned,' Renark said tiredly. 'What did *you* find out?'

'Not much of anything definite. The eleven planets are called a variety of names by a variety of human and non-human people. There are a million theories about the Shifter's nature, mainly based on folk-lore and superstition. They say the Thron were here first and might be native to the system. This could explain some of their resentment of alien ships entering.'

'Anything else?'

'There's some race called, colloquially, the "jelly-smellies", who are supposed to know the history of the multiverse. There's a planet called Ragged Ruth which is supposed to be the epitome of Hell in this hellish system.'

'That seems to confirm what Mary told me,' he nodded.

Talfryn came in. His body was loose, worn out. He sat down on the couch.

Renark paused for a moment.

'There are questions which we've *got* to answer. And we can't take our time getting those answers.

'Why does the Shifter follow this orbit? *How* does it do it? If we can discover the principle, there may be a chance of adapting it to build ships to evacuate our galaxy. The logic—if that's the word—is abhorrent to us, but it must be mastered. Are all the universes contracting at the same time, I wonder?'

He asked this last question almost hesitantly, bringing it into the open for the first time.

'If so, there is virtually no chance of evacuation. On the other hand, what we discover may enable us to . . .'

Klein laughed: 'To stop a universe in its natural course of decay or reorganisation? No, Renark!'

'Yes, Klein—if that has to be done!'

'What the hell are we all talking about?' Talfryn said tiredly from the couch. 'We're only three men—against the natural universe. Not to mention the unnatural universe—this terrible place.'

He shook his head. 'Frankly, the little information I've picked up makes me feel helpless, useless, ineffectual in the face of what's happening. I feel ready to give up, not to fight against something that is, judging by all the facts, an immense and inescapable movement of the forces of nature which must logically result in the end of the human race—of all organic life both in our universe, and in others. The human race has had its day—we might as well face it. If you can answer that, Renark, I'd be grateful . . .'

Suddenly, Renark didn't want Talfryn with him any more.

'I doubt if I could give you an answer which would satisfy you,' he said sadly. 'You're fatalistic. And a fatalist, if you'll forgive me, is also a misanthropist.

'The quality which humanity has, unlike any other form of life in our universe, is its power to control nature. It is the mark of *homo sapiens* that he has, for millennia, refused to let his environment control him to any real extent. He has adapted to it, adapted it, conquered it. This imminent disaster facing the race is on a larger scale—but the rule still applies. In this case we may be forced to leave our environment and start to work adapting to, and controlling, a new one. If Man can do that, he will have proved for ever his right and his reason for existence!'

Talfryn, taken aback by the force of Renark's reply, couldn't answer. He shook his head again and remained broodingly silent. Renark had sensed the man's weakness like a mechanic senses that a piece of equipment, driven beyond its inherent endurance, is due to fail.

So he said: 'Then you'd better stay here.'

Talfryn nodded. 'I've failed you, Renark. But, honestly, it's too big—far too big. Some of us can be optimistic for just so long. But facts must be faced.'

'Facts can be altered,' Renark said, turning away.

'You're giving up?' Asquiol blinked. 'Why?'

'I'm a creature of circumstance,' said Talfryn with a bitter half-smile. He got up and left the room.

Asquiol turned to Renark.

'Why has he done that? Is there something I don't know about?'

'Let's hope so,' Renark said quietly.

He watched his friend who, disturbed and disorientated, turned to look for a long moment at Willow.

Her eyes began to fill with tears.

'I couldn't face it,' she said. 'Not any more—not after what we just went through . . .'

'You've stopped loving me, is that it?'

'Oh, no, Asquiol—I'll always love you. You . . . you could stay here with me.'

Asquiol looked sharply at Renark.

'We go to Thron,' he said.

'If you wish to come.'

'Look after yourself, Willow,' said Asquiol. 'I may return —who knows?' And he walked away from her.

He and Renark left the room, left the building and the city and made for the pads, for their black ship, bound for horror and perhaps death.

'He was a fool,' said Willow calmly to Klein. 'There are many who refuse their responsibilities. Fooling themselves they search for a 'higher ideal.' He was a fool.'

'What are responsibilities?' said Klein laconically. 'He knows. Responsibility, my dear, is another word for self-survival.'

She looked at Klein uncomprehendingly.

'I wish he had stayed,' she said.

FIVE

Renark flung over the ship's master-switch, bringing the whole complicated vessel to life.

He could not be satisfied with thoughts and theories now. He wanted decisive and constant action—dynamic action which would bring him to a source that would answer the questions crowding his mind.

As he charted his course to Thron, he remembered something and turned to Asquiol sitting moodily in the gunnery seat, staring at his instruments.

'Did you ever know of Mary the Maze before you came here?' he asked.

Silently Asquiol shook his head.

Renark shrugged. He felt badly for his friend, but couldn't afford to let his personal emotions influence his chosen course of action.

From what he had gathered, fewer laws than ever applied in the interplanetary space of the Shifter than on the planets themselves. Therefore he was going to have difficulty in simply navigating the comparatively small area of space between them and Thron.

He said without turning, 'Once in space I must not be disturbed, and am relying on you to perform all necessary functions other than the actual piloting of the spaceship. I have to anchor my mind to Thron, and must steer the ship through altering dimensions as well as space and time. Therefor, in the event of attack you must be ready, must meet it as best you can. But I will not be able to afford to know. Do you understand?'

'Let's get started, for God's sake,' he said impatiently.

'And don't be too ready with those anti-neutron cannon,' he said as he pressed the take-off button.

The ship throbbed spacewards.

And then they hit horror!

Chaos

It had no business to exist. It defied every instinctively accepted law that Renark knew.

Turmoil

It was fantastically beautiful. But, as far as he was concerned, it had to be ignored, mastered or destroyed, because it was wrong, evil—unlawful.

Agony

The ship coursed through the myriad, multi-dimensional currents that swirled and whirled and howled about it, that rent the sanity of the two brave men who battered at it, cursed it and, in controlling themselves, managed somehow to stave off the worst effects.

Terror

They had no business to exist here. They knew it, but they refused to compromise. They made the disorder of the tiny universe bend to their courage, to their strength and the wills, creating a pocket of order in the screaming wrongness of unchained creation.

Temptation

They had nothing but their pitiful knowledge that they were human beings—intelligent, reasoning beings capable of transcending the limits which the universe had striven to set upon them. They *refused;* they fought, they used their minds as they had never used them, found reserves of reason where none had previously been.

And, at last, because they were forced to, they used every resource of the human mind which had lain dormant since man had created 'human nature' as an excuse to let his animal nature order his life.

Now they rejected this and Renark steered the ship through the malevolent currents of the unnatural area of space and howled his challenge to it. And the three words *'I am human!'* became his mental war-cry as he used his skill to control the metal vessel plunging on the random spatial and temporal currents and forcing its way through blazing horror towards the angry world of Thron.

All about him, Renark was aware of other dimensions which seemed to lie in wait for his ship, to trap it, to stop it from ever reaching its goal. But he avoided them and concentrated all his powers on keeping a course for Thron.

Four hours the two men fought against insanity, fought the craziness that had turned Mary the Maze into an idiot.

Then, at last, Thron appeared on the laser. Weak, trembling but exuberant, Renark coasted the spaceship into Thron's atmosphere and, although the brooding planet offered new dangers of a more tangible kind, it was with relief and hope that he arrived there.

They could not speak to one another just then. But both were conscious of the welding companionship which had come about during their journey.

They had been fused together, these two men, by mutually shared horror and victory.

Breathing deeply, Renark dropped the ship down and began a cautious reconnaisance of the planet.

Apart from one domed city at the Northern Pole, it appeared deserted. There were cities, certainly, but uninhabited. They picked up no signals, their scanners observed no obvious signs of life. Where were the ferocious Thron? Surely not all at the small city on the Northern Pole?

'The hell with it,' Renark said. 'Let's go right in and see what happens. I've staked everything so far on one throw, and haven't, as yet, lost by it. Are you willing?'

'I thought *I* was supposed to be reckless,' Asquiol smiled. 'Good. We can land in that big square we saw in the largest city.'

Renark nodded agreement, adjusted the controls of the ship and flew in over the big city. He brought it flaming down on the hard, rocky substance of the city square.

They landed to find only silence.

'Shall we disembark?' Asquiol asked.

'Yes. There's a locker over there, beside you. pen it, will you?'

Asquiol swung the door back and raised his eyebrows. There was a small armoury of hand-guns in the locker. Renark had never been known to carry or use any weapon designed to kill.

'Give me the anti-neutron beamer you see there,' Renark said.

Asquiol didn't question Renark but took the holstered gun from the place and handed it over. Renark looked at it strangely.

'Desperate measures,' he said softly. 'I have little sympathy at the moment with the Thron, although they may have justifiable reasons for their seemingly unreasoning belligerence. But our mission transcends my moral code, much as I hate to admit such a thing possible, and our lives are, as far as the human race is concerned, important.'

'Let's go,' said Asquiol.

Renark sighed. They suited up and took the elevator to the airlock.

Although bizzare and obviously created by alien intelligence, Renark and Asquiol could work out the function of most of the buildings and machines they observed as they padded through the deserted streets of the apparently deserted city.

But they couldn't explain why the city was deserted, where the inhabitants had gone. Obviously they had not been gone for any length of time, for there were no signs of erosion or encroaching nature.

With his mind, Renark quested around, searching the buildings for life, but he could only sense peculiar disturbances in the temporal and spatial layers spreading out beyond the Shifter continuum.

Life hovered out there like a ghost, sometimes apparently close, sometimes further away. It was weird.

They toured the city and were just returning to the square where the ship reared when something happened.

'God, I feel sick . . .' Asquiol said, screwing up his eyes.

Renark felt the same. He had momentary double vision. He saw faint shadows flickering at the edge of the structures about them, shadows of the same shape, size and appearance as the more solid buildings and machines. These shadows seemed to merge with the material structures—and all at once the city was alive, inhabited.

The place was suddenly full of doglike, six-legged beings using four legs for motion and two as hands.

The Thron!

Shocked, they pulled their pistols from their holsters and

backed towards the ship as the Thron saw the humans in their midst.

All was consternation.

Thron soldiers levelled weirdly curled tubes at the two men, levelled them—and fired. The humans were flung to the ground as their suit-screens absorbed or repelled the the worst of the charges.

'Shoot back or we've had it!' Renark yelled.

They raised themselves on their bellies and fired their own dreadful weapons.

Beams of dancing anti-matter went spreading towards the Thron troops, met them, made contact and seethed into their bodies.

Those bodies imploded, crushing inwards and turning to miniscule specks of shattered matter before vanishing entirely. The backlash shivered against the humans' protective suits. And the beams waltzed on, fading slightly as they progressed, entered one group after another, destroying wherever they touched, whether organic or inanimate matter, until their power faded. Only a few Thron were left in the immediate area.

'They don't seem ready to talk,' Asquiol said sardonically over the suit radio. 'What now, Renark?'

'Back to the ship, for the meantime.'

Inside the control cabin their communications equipment was making all sorts of noises. Asquiol attempted to tune it in and eventually succeeded in getting a regular series of high-frequency signals which he could not quite interpret as being coded signals or actual speech. He brought the pitch down lower and realised with astonishment that he was listening to stilted Terran. Renark was busy keeping the scanners trained on the Thron, who were coming out into the open around the square again. But he listened.

'*Beware the Thron . . . Beware the Thron . . . Beware the Thron . . .*'

Whether it was a warning or a threat, he couldn't tell. Asquiol said, careful to adjust his outgoing signal to the frequency involved: 'Who are you? I am receiving you.'

'We are enemies of the Thron. We are the Shaarn, whose ancestors consigned the Thron to this existence. But they have machines which you are not equipped against—forces which will hurl you out of this system altogether and into Limbo. Take off immediately and head for the Northern

Pole. We saw you pass over us but have not, until now, been able to discover your means of communication and the form it takes. We apologise.'

'How can we trust them?' Asquiol asked.

'The frying pan or the fire—it makes no difference,' Renark replied. 'I'm lifting off. Tell them we're coming.'

Asquiol relayed the message.

'You must hurry,' the Shaarn spokesman said, 'for we are small and have few defensive devices against the Thron. You must reach our city before they do, since we will have but a short time to spare to let you in and close our barrier again.'

'Have it ready—we're coming,' said Asquiol.

The ship soared upwards again, levelled off and headed at high speed for the polar region.

They made it in under a minute. They saw the dome flicker and fade, entered its confines as it closed over them again, and came down gently on a small landing field within the city. It was more a town, with few buildings taller than three stories, encompassing a small area compared with the expanse of the Thron cities. Overhead they observed the Thron ships come rushing over the polar city and were half blinded by the bolts of energy which sprayed the force-dome above them.

They stayed where they were and waited to be contacted.

Eventually the communications equipment spoke: 'I am pleased that we were successful. There is no point in waiting until the Throns have expended their rage. The force-shield will hold off their most ferocious attacks. We are sending out a vehicle for your assistance. Please take it to the city when you are ready to do so.'

A few moments later a small air-carriage, open-topped and made of thin, golden metal, floated up to the ship and hovered by its airlock.

'Well, let's see if these Shaarn are friendly or not,' said Renark.

They descended to the airlock, passed through it and entered the little airboat which turned on its axis and returned to the city at a more leisurely speed.

Renark felt fairly confident, from what Mary the Maze had said, that these people would be friendly.

They entered the city proper and the airboat cruised downwards, landing gently outside the entrance to a small, un-ornamented, unpretentious building.

Two figures came out. They were dog-like, having six apendages. Asquiol gasped and instinctively reached for his pistol in an unthinking response. Then he saw that these creatures, so like the Thron, were unarmed, and he calmed himself.

The Shaarn, like the Thron, were extremely pleasing to the human eye—perhaps because they looked so alike to friendly dogs.

The two figures, with peaceful gestures, beckoned Renark and Asquiol to leave the airboat. They did so. They passed through a series of simply furnished rooms containing no recognisable equipment, and out into a courtyard which, like the city, was covered with an iridescent force-dome.

Here was a laser transceiver not unlike their own. One of the Shaarn went up to it and spoke into the transmitter. It took them several moments to tune into the humans' suit wave-lengths and, for an instant, before they adjusted their own controls, they were blasted with the high-pitched noises they had heard before.

Then the Shaarn spokesman said: 'We regret, sincerely, that our welcome could not have extended to the whole planet, but as you will have realised, we control little of it. I am Naro Nuis and this is my wife Zeni Ouis. You are Renark Jon and Asquiol of Pompeii, I believe.'

'That's so, but how did you know?' Renark replied.

'We were forced—and you must forgive us—to intrude on your minds in order to discover the means to build the communications equipment. We are telepaths, I am afraid . . .'

'Then why the need for the laser?'

'We had no idea how you would take telepathic inter-ference in your minds, and it is against our code to intrude except in the direst emergencies.'

'I should have thought that's just what we *were* in,' Asquiol said somewhat rudely.

'I see,' said Renark. 'Well, as far as I am concerned, tele-pathic communication would be preferable. We have tele-paths among our own race.'

'So be it,' Naro Nuis said.

'You have obviously some important reason for braving

the dangers of Thron,' said a voice in Renark's skull, 'but we avoided investigating it. Perhaps we can help?'

'Thank you,' Renark said. 'Firstly, I am curious to learn why the Throns are so belligerent; secondly, whether it is true that your race was the first to come to this system. Much hangs on what I learn from you.' He told the Shaarn how his race faced annihilation.

The alien appeared to deliberate. At length he 'pathed:

'Would you object if we intruded still further on your minds for a while by means of a telepathic link? By this method you will see something of the history of the Shaarn and will discover how this system originally took this some-what unusual orbit through the multi-dimensional universe.'

'What do you say, Renark?' Asquiol's voice came over the suit-phone.

'I think the suggestion is excellent.'

They were led into a semi-darkened room where food and drink were served to them. They felt relaxed for the first time in ages.

'This place is simply to aid your receptivity to what we are about to do.'

'And what is that?'

'We are going to reconstruct for you the history of the war between the Shaarn and the Thron. The history began many millennia ago, when our ancestors were completing their explorations of our own space-time galaxy . . .'

At Naro Nuis' request they blanked their minds, and the history began . . .

SIX

They were the golden children of the galaxy. The Shaarn—the searchers, the wanderers, the enquirers. They were the magnificent bringers of gifts, bestowers of wisdom, dealers of justice. In their great star-travelling ships they brought the concept of mercy and law to the planets of their galaxy and formed order out of chaos, cut justice from the stuff of chance.

The Shaarn hurled their ships inwards to the Hub, out-wards towards the Rim.

Proud, wise and merciful, self-confident and self-critical, they spread their sons to inhabit planets in many different systems. The laughing darlings of an ancient culture, they poured outwards, always searching.

The Shaarn ships sang and hurtled through the bewildering regions of hyperspace, avoiding war, recognising privacy, but bringing their wisdom and knowledge to anyone requesting it. They had come, also to accept that all intelligent races took the same form as themselves.

The mighty Shaarn were cynics and idealists, innocent and ancient—and their ships coursed further towards the worlds of the Rim.

The starship *Vondel,* captained by Roas Rui, burst into normal space half a light-year from a binary star the Shaarn called Yito. Around Yito circled eleven worlds, each following a wider orbit than the next—eleven mysteries which Roas Rui and his crew of scientists and sorcerers regarded with excitement and curiosity. Eleven balls of chemicals and vegetation, organic and inorganic life. Would they find intelligence? New concepts, new knowledge? Roas Rui hoped that they would.

The Shaarn, in their early days of space-travel, had known fear when encountering foreign cultures, but those times were gone. In their power and their confidence, they were unable to conceive of a race greater than their own, a technology more highly developed. On some worlds near the Rim they had come across traces of a star-roving people, but the traces were incredibly ancient and pointed to a long-dead race—their ancestors, perhaps—who had travelled the stars and then degenerated. Thus, it was not with fear that Roas Rui regarded the fourth world nearest Yito when his ship, its reactor idling, went into orbit around it.

Roas Rui reared himself effortlessly on to his four hind limbs in order to see better the purple-clouded world which now filled the viewing-screen. His shaggy, dog-like head craned towards the screen and his mouth curved downwards in an expression of pure pleasure. He turned his head and showed his long, slim teeth to emphasise his delight.

'It's a huge planet, Medwov Dei,' he released to his lieutenant who stood by the screen control board, manoeuvring dials in order to bring the world into closed perspective.

Medwov Dei thought, without moving his head, 'The gravity is almost identical to that of Shaarn.'

Rui thought. 'Noui Nas was right in his hunch again. He always picks the planet which most closely approximates Shaarn in gravity and atmosphere. He's one of the best sorcerers we have in the Division.'

Medwov made a clicking sound with his mouth to indicate agreement. He was very big, the largest member of the crew and every inch of five feet high. He was dedicated to the Exploratory Division, even more than the other members. With regard to his work, he was a fanatic, probably due to the fact that, because of his immense size, he had little success with the female Shaarn. At least he, personally, blamed his height, but it was well known that, as a young cadet, he had once killed a domestic beast in anger. Naturally, this had led to his near-ostracism and had precluded his ever rising above the rank of Lieutenant. Medwov inhaled wetly and continued to work at the control panel, deliberately blocking his mind to any but the most urgent thoughts which might emanate from his commander.

Almost childishly, Roas Rui laughed the high-pitched whine of the Shaarn. His excitement mounted as he directed his two pilots to prepare for descent on to the planet's surface.

'Prepare defence screens.' He sent out the traditional commands as a matter of course. Some of his orders were obeyed by the control operators before he even thought of them. 'Switch to gravity-resisters.' Machines moaned delicately throughout the huge bulk of the starship. 'Descend to two thousand feet.'

The *Vondel* plunged through the atmosphere of the new planet and hovered two thousand feet above its surface. Now the screens showed a vast landscape of forest land comprised predominantly of waving indigo fronds which stretched like a sea in all directions, broken occasionally by clumps of taller vegetation coloured in varying shades of blue. It was beautiful. Roas Rui's long body shook with emotion as he beheld it. To the Shaarn all new planets were beautiful.

'Begin testing,' he said.

The computers began their intricate job of classifying all the components of the planet. At the same time, the sorcerers began to put themselves swiftly into trance-state, seeking to discover intelligent life of any kind, whether natural or supernatural, and also its attitude or potential attitude to the Exploratory Division.

The findings of computers and sorcerers were relayed instantly to Roas Rui, himself now in semi-trance. Both parts of his brain received the information and assembled it into an ever-increasing, detailed picture of the newly discovered planet.

Woui Nas:

I have found a mind. Bewildered. Uncertain. Passive. More minds. As before. New! Mind. High intelligence. Anger. Controlled. Urge to destroy very strong: directed at (possible) Rulers or Representatives. New! Mind. Low IQ. Misery. Bewildered. Passive. New! Something bad. Very bad. Evil here, but am finding resistance to probes.

Pause . . .

Power. Evil. Great resistance to probes. Am formed to fight or retreat. Require orders!

Pause . . .

Repeat. Require orders!

Roas Rui beamed a message to the controllers to continue recording the data and concentrated all his attention on making a full link with Woui Nas, who had 'pathed the urgent request.

'I am with you now, Woui Nas. Can you bring me in?'

'Unprecedented reaction, captain. Please absorb.'

Roas Rui could sense the frightened amazement of Woui Nas as he submerged himself in the other's mind and allowed the old sorcerer to guide him outwards towards the source of the emanations. Almost instantaneously, he felt the aura of disgusting malevolence, coupled with an intelligence more powerful than his own. Roas Rui was one of the most intelligent members of his race—his capacity for absorbing and relating knowledge was tremendous—but he had found more than his match in the mind which now sensed the presence of his own.

Roas Rui, under the direction of Woui Nas, probed further into the mind which he had contacted. He probed while his senses shrieked with danger and urged him to retreat.

Suddenly his brain throbbed as a thought came savagely from the contacted entity: *'Get out! We intend to destroy you, intruders.'*

There was no attempt to ask questions of the explorers. No tinge of curiosity. An order—and a statement.

Roas Rui and Woui Nas retreated from the malevolence and separated minds.

'What now?' Woui Nas asked from his cabin, a quarter of a mile away from the control room where Roas Rui sat shaking.

'Incredible,' the captain said. 'Quite unprecedented, as you remarked. There is a force here to equal the Shaarn—even to better it. But the *evil!*'

'I must admit that, as we neared the planet, I sensed it,' Woui Nas informed the captain. 'But it was difficult then to define it. These entities are capable of blocking off our most powerful probes.'

'Our ancestors would have been far more careful when making a new planet-fall,' Ross Rui said grimly. 'We are becoming too complacent, Brother Sorcerer.'

'*Were*,' Woui Nas remarked dryly. 'Perhaps this is the kind of shock our people need.'

'Possibly,' Roas Rui agreed. 'But now we are in danger of turning our immediate peril into a philosophical problem. Since this contact is unprecedented, and since the regulations state categorically that we should obey any culture which demands that we leave its environs, I would suggest to you that a group makes contact immediately with Headquarters on Shaarn and asks for instructions.'

'And meanwhile?' Woui Nas enquired.

'I do not wish to be destroyed. And neither, I think, do any other members of the ship's complement.' He beamed a quick order to his pilots. 'We are returning to Shaarn. This is an emergency.' He knew that his pilots would need no further orders.

Swiftly, the *Vondel* climbed into deep space and merged into hyperspace.

So the initial contact between the Shaarn and the Thron was made.

Another millennia of ignorance of each other's existence, the exploratory team which had come to a Thron-dominated world brought the two mighty cultures into contact at last. It was inevitable.

And the war between Shaarn and Thron was also inevitable.

It was not a war like most wars. It did not hinge on economics. It only partially hinged on conflicting ideologies. It was simply that the Thron refused to tolerate the presence

61

in the galaxy of another intelligent race, physically like themselves and almost as powerful.

They intended to destroy the Shaarn. To obliterate completely all traces of their civilisation. The Thron had not concentrated so much on the building of starships, but it did not take them long to build ships which almost equalled those of the Shaarn.

Thron controlled an Empire comprising twenty-six systems. The Thron themselves were comparatively few in number—but they had total dominance over their subject planets.

The Federation of Shaarn comprised some fifty systems and three hundred planets upon which intelligent races, like themselves, existed. When Shaarn informed them of the impending war, one hundred and sixty-two of those planets elected to join with the Shaarn. The rest claimed neutrality.

The war progressed. It was vicious and dreadful. And a month after it had begun the first planet was destroyed by the Thron—a neutral planet. And all life was destroyed with the planet.

Realising the danger was great, but unable to consider an alternative to continuing the struggle, the Shaarn directed their scientists to devise a means of stopping the war so that no more destruction of life should take place.

The scientists devised a means of removing the Thron from the galaxy, even from the very universe—a means, if it worked as they hoped, of forever exiling that malevolent and evil people.

They discovered the continuum-warp device which, they believed, would be capable of hurling the eleven Thron home-worlds out of their continuum and into another. This would efficiently halt the Thron's insensate aims of ruling the galaxy.

So a squadron of ships, each armed with the device, reached the Thron home system of Yito and directed their beams on to the planets and their sun.

At first they succeeded only in shifting the planets through space, altering the position around the binary, resulting in the equidistant position they now occupied. The Thron retaliated and the Shaarn hurled the Thron warships effectively into another space-time continuum. Returning their attention to the system, they blasted it with warp rays time after time and, quite suddenly, it was gone—vanished from the Shaarn's space-time into another. The war was over.

But, as it happened, the Shaarn had not been entirely successful in their plan since the system kept right on travelling through the dimensions, eventually establishing an orbit which it still followed. Not only this, but most of the Shaarn ships were caught up in the vortex they had created and were drawn, by means of the force they had themselves released, after the Shifter.

They attempted, desperately, to return to their own space-time but, for some reason, it was now blocked, not only to them but to the Shifter itself. The system could never pass through the Shaarn's space-time again.

The Thron, demoralised and bewildered, did not offer a threat of immediate counter-attack for they were busily consolidating on their fortress world, abandoning their slaves to any fate that came.

The Shaarn were able to land their ships, establishing a small, well-protected city at the Northern Pole of a planet they called Glanii. Here they remained for ages, vainly attempting to devise a means of returning to their own system.

Later the Thron, too, came to Glanii, where they could be nearer their hated enemies.

The Thron eventually learned what had happened to them and also began work on the problem. They invented a machine which could fling them and all their artifacts through the multi-dimensional space-time streams to their home continuum and exact vengeance on the Shaarn. So far they had not been unsuccessful.

This explained why Renark and Asquiol had found the planet apparently deserted of Thron, who at the time of their arrival had been attempting another jump through the dimensions.

The war between the Thron and the representatives of the Shaarn had become stalemate, both races concentrating most of their energies on attempts to return to their home continuum. So it had been for millennia, with the Thron, resenting further encroachments on their sundered territory, attempting to destroy any newcomers who came, like vultures, opportunistically to the Shifter system.

And that, to the date of Renark's coming, was briefly the history of the Sundered Worlds . . .

Renark was in a calmer frame of mind when the experience was over. At last he was no longer working in the dark—he had definite, conclusive facts to relate to his questions and was confident that the Shaarn would supply him with further useful information.

Naro Nuis telepathed discreetly: 'I hope the history was of some use to you, Renark Jon.'

'Of great use—but I gather you are unable to supply me with any detailed information of the dimension-warping device.'

'Unfortunately, that is so. From what we can gather, the continua-warp, operating as it did by means of certain laws discovered in the Shaarn continuum, will not work in the same way from outside the continuum. I believe this was deliberately done by our scientists in order that the Thron would never be able to return.'

'I'm surprised that by this time you haven't joined forces with the Thron, since you seem to have a common aim.'

'Not so. In fact, this is our main point of contention these days. The Thron are determined to regain our original universe, whereas that is the last thing we want. We will be pleased to halt the progress of the Shifter in *any* continuum but our own, and this would destroy, for ever, their chance to continue the war.' The alien sighed—a surprisingly human sound. 'It may be that the Shifting mechanism is an irreversible process. In that case our efforts are hopeless. But we do not think so.'

Renark was bitterly disappointed. If the beings who engendered the Shift no longer understood how it operated, this was logically the end of the trail. But he would not admit to himself that there was nothing more he could do. That was unthinkable.

He rose to his feet, his mind working intensely, busily forming the recent knowledge into the kind of pattern best suited to his present needs. Well, there was time yet. He had to be optimistic—there was no turning back. He refused to accept any factors other than those he could use objectively. Somewhere in this system . . .

They left the chamber and made for the ship. On the way, Renark noticed signs of animated work in a large, low-slung building with open-hangar-type doors. It struck him as out of tune with the millennia-long deadlock of which he had just learned.

He remarked on this to Naro Nuis. The alien immediately responded with interest.

'That is the result of a long period of research. We are now building equipment with which we hope to halt the Shifter system.'

Renark stared in amazement. 'What? After the story of gloom you have just told us?'

'I told you our experiments continued,' Naro Nuis replied, puzzled. 'Soon we will begin ferrying the equipment into space, to take it as near to the suns as possible.'

'And yet you still claim to have no knowledge of the Shift principle!' Renark's excitement was mounting at the thought that the creature had been lying.

'That is so,' Naro Nuis told him. 'We have despaired of ever discovering the principle behind the phenomenon. But, with any luck, we think we might bring it to a stop, even though we don't understand it.'

He added: 'This is the culmination of a very long series of experiments. Very long. If we succeed, we shall not need to know, since the phenomenon will have vanished.'

Renark's sudden hope dissipated. 'And what are your chances of succeeding?'

Naro Nuis paused before answering. 'The expedition is fraught with dangers. Our long absence from space has lost us some of our skills in interplanetary flight.'

'What of the Thron? Do they know of your plans?'

'They have some inkling, of course. They will try to stop us. There will be a great battle.'

Renark continued the walk to his ship. 'When do you plan to lift this equipment off?'

'In half a revolution of the planet.'

He stopped abruptly. 'Then I must ask one favour.'

'What is that?'

'Delay your experiment. Give me time to find out what I must know.'

'We cannot.'

There was no arguing with the Shaarn. His tone was uncompromising.

Naro Nuis explained: 'How can we be sure that you will have even a chance of success in your endeavour? Every moment we delay means that our chances of stopping the Shifter and holding off the Thron are lessened.'

'But the future of my entire race depends upon me!'

'Does it? Have you not taken it upon yourself presumptuously to save your fellows? Perhaps the process you described is natural—perhaps the members of your race will accept that they are to perish along with their universe. As for us, there is no need to delay and we must act quickly. The Thron—when they are not attempting to jump through the dimensions—patrol the planet in their ships. As soon as we begin ferrying the equipment there will be a battle. We will have to work speedily and hold off the Thron at the same time.'

'I see,' Renark said bitterly.

Later, Asquiol said: 'But what if you did stop the Shifter? Supposing you stopped it in a universe like the one we have just left? You would be destroyed along with the rest.'

'That is true—but the chances of that happening are not very great. We must risk it.'

'Then you will not wait?'

'No,' Naro Nuis said again, regretfully. 'Your hopes of success are slim. Ours are better. You must understand our position. We have been trying to stop the Shifter for thousands of years. Would you call a halt to your progress on behalf of a race you never heard of—which, according to only two of its members, was in some kind of danger?'

'I might,' Renark said.

'Not after thousands of years,' said Asquiol. 'Not that long.'

Naro Nuis's thoughts came gently. 'You are welcome to stay with us if you wish.'

'Thanks,' Renark said harshly, 'but we don't have much time.'

'I think your efforts will be wasted,' the Shaarn pathed, 'but since you are so anxious to find help you might go to the world of the Ekiversh.'

'Ekiversh?'

'The Evikersh are intelligent metazoa who have a fully-developed race-memory. They gave us some help in building the machine with which we intend to stop the Shifter. They have lived so long that their knowledge is very great. They are good-natured, friendly and, because of their structure and type, live on the only planet in the system which is not in some way torn by strife. The Thron could learn something from the Ekiversh but, in their arrogance, they would not deign to do so. We have not often visited them, for whenever we leave our city the wrath of the Thron is turned upon us. But we have made telepathic communication when certain favourable laws have applied, for short periods, in the system.'

'Can you point out their planet on my chart?'

'With pleasure.'

Naro Nuis accompanied them aboard their ship, looking around him with pleasure and curiosity.

'A bizarre craft,' he said.

'Not by our standards.' Renark produced the chart and the alien bent over it, studying the figures marked there. At last he pointed. 'There.'

'Thanks,' said Renark.

'Let's get started, shall we?' Asquiol drummed his fingers.

'The Thron will be awaiting you when you leave here,' Naro Nuis said. 'Are you sure you want to risk it?'

'What else could we do?' Renark was close to anger.

The alien turned away from him.

Asquiol shouted at Naro Nuis:

'Haven't you any idea what you will do if you stop the Shifter? You could strand us here with no means of saving our people—no means of going back, even if we did find the information we need. You *can't* begin your experiments yet!'

'We must.'

Renark put his hand on Asquiol's arm. 'We must get to Ekiversh as soon as possible and see what we can learn before the Shaarn succeed in stopping the Shifter in orbit.'

'Then I had better leave,' Naro Nuis said sadly.

With mixed emotions, Renark said goodbye to the alien, thanking him for his help but aware that this pleasant people were about to conduct an experiment which—if it was successful —would shatter his own hopes of learning enough from the Shifter to be able to return to his own universe and save humanity.

Renark sat in the control seat, tensed. Asquiol fidgeted in his own seat by the gunnery panel.

Suddenly the force-dome over the city flickered, flashed bright orange and boiled backwards, leaving a gap. Renark's finger smashed down on the firing switch. The ship trembled, screamed and lifted.

Then they were through the gap in the screen, whining up through the clouds towards the madness of the Shifter's space.

Thron ships spotted them instantly and came flashing in their direction.

Asquiol didn't wait for Renark's order this time. As they sped into deep space, he fired.

The Thron ships flickered away from the cold, searing stream of anti-neutrons which Asquiol, in his desperation, had dared again to employ, and which their instruments told them meant instant disruption. Even so, some vessels were caught for an instant in the periphery of the deadly flow, and must have suffered for it. Anti-neutrons, possessing no electrical charge, could not be stopped by any energy screen.

Asquiol could almost see the Thron licking their wounds.

He had hoped that this first exchange would frighten the attackers badly enough to give Renark time to make a clean getaway. But the Thron had the advantage of being able to manoeuvre in Shifter space. Renark gritted his teeth as he piled on power and plunged into the billowy *twistiness* which this region presented to his mind. It was almost like piloting a boat through mad, storm-tossed seas.

But they were seas that intruded into the mind.

The Thron came after them, and Asquiol saw them somersault preparatory to firing. He hesitated, reluctant to use his weapon a second time. Then great slams of force hit them.

The ship skidded and bucked. 'Don't pussyfoot, Asquiol,' Renark roared uncharacteristically. 'Let them have it!'

Asquiol clung to the firming arm of the anti-neutron gun. Blindly, he turned up the density to maximum and sprayed space. Phantasmal green flares showed, on the screen before him, where he scored hits.

Renark closed his eyes and concentrated hard on the piloting. The collapse of atomic structures on a large scale was not a pleasant experience for a space senser.

After that, the surviving Thron ships withdrew. There was silence in the cabin of Renark's ship for some time.

A few hours later Renark made a quick mental exploration. He found what he'd expected. The Shaarn had begun the first stages of the experiment. There was evidence of fierce fighting near the Thron planet, and somewhere sunward a sizeable installation was being set up.

He probed further. At present the Shaarn were unmolested, but not for long. A large fleet was assembled an hour's journey away, and would soon no doubt do much to impede the progress of the Shaarn's labours. In spite of the friendliness shown him by his hosts, Renark began to regret the Thron warships destroyed by Asquiol.

Soon, Renark felt, he would be gaining a complete picture of the workings of the multiverse. There were other things he wished to know and he had a feeling that if he lived he would know them soon.

Once again they were experiencing the chaotic and bewildering currents of outer space. But this time there was little emotional reaction, for their self-confidence was strong.

But Renark still had to fight to keep the ship on course in the stormy, lawless and random flowings of time and space, skimming the ship over them like a stone over water, through myriad sterechronia, through a thousand million twists of the spatial flow, to come finally to Ekiversh . . .

SEVEN

Immediately they landed on the peaceful oxygen planet, tiny, polite threads of thought touched their minds, asked questions.

Responding to the delicacy of the impressions, Renark and Asquiol made it clear that they wished to contact the Ekiversh as the Shaarn had suggested. They remained in the spaceship, pleased to see the light green chlorophyll-bearing plants which were not unlike Earth's.

At last there appeared outside the ship what at first appeared to be a heaving mass of semi-transparent jelly. Disgusted, Renark was repelled by the sight and Asquiol said:

'The jelly-smellies. Remember I told you they were some sort of legend on Entropium? Metazoa—*ugh!*'

A voice in Asquiol's head said humbly: 'We are deeply sorry that our physical appearance should not appeal. Perhaps this will be a better form.'

Then the whole mass reared up and slowly transformed itself into the shape of a giant man—a giant man comprised of hundreds of gelatinous metazoa.

Renark could not decide which form was least unattractive, but he blocked the idea out of his mind and said instead:

'We have come to converse with you on matters of philosophy and practical importance to us and our race. May we leave our ship? It would be good to breathe real air again.'

But the metazoan giant replied regretfully: 'It would be unwise, for though we absorb oxygen as you do, the waste gases we exhale are unpleasing to your sense of smell.'

'The "jelly-smellies," ' Renark said to Asquiol. 'That explains their name.'

'We were informed that you are equipped with race-memory, that in effect you are immortal,' Renark thought tentatively at the glutinous giant.

'That is so. Our great experience, as you may know, was to have witnessed, in the early days of our race, the dance of a galaxy.'

'Forgive me, but I don't understand the implications of that,' Renark said. 'Could you perhaps explain what you mean?'

'It was believed,' said metazoa, 'that those whom we call the Doomed Folk had passed away in a distant galaxy in our original universe, and that galaxy—which had known great strife—was quiet again in readiness for the Great Turn which would be the beginning of a new cycle in its long life. We and other watchers in nearby galaxies saw it shift like a smoky monster, saw it curl and writhe and its suns and planets pour in ordered patterns around the Hub and out around the Rim, reforming their ranks in preparation.

'The Dance of the Stars was a sight to destroy all but the noblest of watchers, for the weaving patterns depicted the Two Truths Which Bear the Third, so that while the galaxy reformed itself to begin a fresh cycle through its particular Time and Space, it also cleansed its sister galaxies of petty spirits and those who thought ignoble thoughts.

'For millions of years, The Dance of the Galaxy progressed —ordered creation, a sight so pleasing to intelligent beings. It gave us much in the way of sensory experiences and also enabled us to develop our philosophy. Please do not ask us to explain it further, for the sight of a galaxy dancing can be defined in no terms possessed by either of us.

'When at last the Dance was over, the Hub began to spin, setting the pattern for the new Cycle. And slowly, from the hub outwards to the Rim, the suns and planets began to turn again in a course that would be unchanged for eons.

'So it began, and so—after time had passed—did its denizens begin to hammer out its marvellous history.

'They came, at length, to our galaxy and, because they were impatient of the philosophical conclusions we had drawn about the nature of the multiverse, set about destroying our ancient race. A few of us fled here, since we abhor violence or knowledge of violence.'

'You witnessed a galaxy re-order itself by its own volition!' Renark sensed at last that his most important question was close to being answered.

'Not, we feel, by its own volition. Our logic has led us, inescapably, to believe that there is a greater force at work —one which created the multiverse for its own purposes. This is not a metaphysical conclusion—we are materialists. But the facts are such that they point to the existence of beings who are, in the true sense, supernatural.'

'And the multiverse—what of that? Does it consist of an infinite number of layers, or . . .?'

'The multiverse is finite. Vast as it is, it has limitations. And beyond those limitations exist—other realities, perhaps.'

Renark was silent. All his life he had accepted the concept of infinity, but even his rapidly developing mind could not quite contain the new concept hovering at the edge of his consciousness.

'We believe,' said the metazoa gently, 'that life as we know it is in an undeveloped, crude state—that you and we represent perhaps the first stage in the creation of entities designed, at length, to transcend the limitations of the multiverse. It has been our function, all of us, to have created some sort of order out of original chaos. There is no such thing, even now, as cause and effect—there is still only cause and coincidence; coincidence and effect. There is no such thing, and this, of course, is obvious to any intelligence. There is no such thing as free will—there is only limited choice. We are limited not only by our environment, but by our psychological condition, by our physical needs—everywhere we turn we are limited. The Ekiversh believe that, though this is true, we can conceive *of* a condition in which this is not so—and perhaps, in time, conceive that condition.'

'I agree,' Renark nodded. 'It is possible to overcome all restrictions if the will is strong enough.'

'That may be so. You have certainly come through more than any other entity—and it has been your spirit which has

71

been the only thing to keep your mind and body co-ordinated for so long. But, if you wish to continue your quest for as far as you can go in a finite universe, you have the worst experience to come.'

'What do you mean?'

'You must go to the lattice planet. There you will meet the dwellers in the Abyss of Reality. Perhaps you have heard of the place as the Hole.'

Yes, Renark had heard the name. He remembered where. Mary had told him about it.

'What exactly is this planet?'

'It does not move through the multiverse in the same way as the rest of the planets in this system, yet in a sense it exists in *all* of them. Pieces of it move in different dimensions, all shifting independently. Sometimes the planet may be fairly complete on random occasions. At other times the planet is full of . . . *gaps* . . . where parts of it have ceased to exist according to the dimensional laws operating in whichever continua the Shifter is in. It is believed that there exists somewhere in this planet a gateway through to a mythical race called The Originators.

'Since you have nowhere else to go, we would suggest that you risk a visit to this planet and attempt to find the gateway, if it exists.'

'Yes, we shall try,' said Renark softly. Then another thought came to him. 'Why isn't this planet, Erkiversh, subject to the same chaotic conditions existing elsewhere?' he asked.

'That is because, before we fled our home universe, we prepared for the conditions which we expected to meet, and we used our skill and knowledge to create a very special organism.'

The glutinous giant seemed to heave its shining body before the next thought came.

'We call it a Conservator. The conservator is simply an object, but an object of a peculiar kind which can only exist under a certain set of laws. In order to maintain its own existence, it conserves these laws for a distance around it. These laws, of course, are those under which we exist and under which you, for the most part, exist also. With a conservator in your ship, you will not experience your earlier difficulties in traversing interplanetary space and, also, you will be less likely to lose your way on the lattice planet which, incidentally, you know of as Roth, or Ragged Ruth.'

'I am grateful,' Renark said. 'The conservator will be of great assistance.' Then another thought occurred to him. 'You are aware of my reason for coming here—because the universe where I belong is contracting. Could not a number of these conservators be built in order to stop the course which my universe is taking?'

'Impossible. Your universe is not contravening any natural laws. The laws which apply to it are bringing about this change. You must discover why this is happening—for everything has a purpose—and discover what part your race is to play in this reorganisation.'

'Very well,' said Renark humbly.

Several of the metazoa detached themselves from the main body and disappeared in the direction of a line of hills, travelling rapidly. 'We go to fetch a conservator,' the pseudo-giant told him.

Renark used the wait to explore his own state of mind. Strangely, without any great strain, he could now accept the enormity of the realisation which had been dawning in him ever since he first came to the Shifter. And he knew now, unquestioningly, that his whole journey, his trials and endeavours, had had, from the beginning, a definite *purpose*— there was logic in the multiverse. The Ekiversh had convinced him. And that purpose, he thought with dawning clarity, transcended his original one—transcended it and yet was part of it!

But there was much more, he felt, to undergo before this new need in him would be consummated. For now he was to undergo the worst part of the journey—to the planet that had sent Mary the Maze insane. Ruth—Ragged Ruth—the Lattice Planet.

The metazoa returned bearing a small globe of a dull ochre colouring. This they placed on the ground, near the airlock of the spaceship.

'We shall leave you now,' the metazoa telepathed, 'but let us wish you knowledge. You Renark and Asquiol are the messengers for the multiverse—you must represent us all if you succeed in reaching the Originators—presuming they exist. You go further towards reality than any other intelligent beings, apart from the dwellers of The Hole, have done before . . .'

Asquiol got into a suit and went outside to collect the

conservator. Renark watched him, his gaze unblinking, his thoughts distant, as he returned and placed the globe on the chart desk beside Renark.

Automatically, Renark prepared himself for take-off, thanked the metazoa and pressed the drive control.

Then they were plunging upwards, cutting a pathway of law through the tumbling insanity of interplanetary space.

But this time there was no need to fight it. The conservator acted just as the Ekiversh had predicted, setting up a field all about itself where its own laws operated. Relieved, they had time to talk.

Asquiol had been taken aback by all the events and information he had received. He said: 'Renark, I'm still bewildered. Why exactly are we going to Roth?'

Renark's mood was detached, his voice sounding far away even to his own ears.

'To save the human race. I am realising now that the means of salvation are of a subtler kind than I previously suspected. That is all.'

'But surely we have lost sight of the original purpose for this mission? More—we are living in a fantasy world. This talk of reality is nonsense!'

Renark was not prepared to argue, only to explain.

'The time has come for the dismantling of fantasies. That is already happening to our universe. Now that we have this one chance of survival we must finally rid ourselves of fantasies and seize that chance!

'For centuries our race has built on false assumptions. If you build a fantasy based on a false assumption and continue to build on such a fantasy, your whole existence becomes a lie which you implant in others who are too lazy or too busy to question its truth.

'In this manner you threaten the very existence of reality, because, by refusing to obey its laws, those laws engulf and destroy you. The human race has for too long been manufacturing convenient fantasies and calling them laws. For ages this was so. Take war, for instance, Politicians *assume* that something is true, *assume* that strife is inevitable, and by building on such false assumptions, lo and behold, they create further wars which they have, ostensibly, sought to prevent.

'We have, until now, accepted too many fantasies as being truths, too many truths as fantasies. And we have one last chance to discover the real nature of our existence. I am prepared to take it!'

'And I.' Asquiol spoke softly, but with conviction. He paused and then added with a faint half-smile: 'Though you must forgive me if I still do not fully comprehend your argument.'

'You'll understand it soon enough if things go right.' Renark smiled broadly. Roth now loomed huge on the laser screens.

With a deliberate lack of reverence, Asquiol commented: 'It looks like a great maggoty cheese, doesn't it?'

In the places seeming like glowing sores, they could see right through the planet. In other places there were *gaps* which jarred the eyes, numbed the mind.

Although they could see vaguely the circular outline, the planet was gashed as though some monstrous worm had chewed at it like a caterpillar on a leaf.

Refusing to let the sight overawe him—though it threatened to—Renark brought his skill as a Guide Senser to bear. Deliberately, yet warily, he probed the mass of the weird planet. Where the *gaps* were, he sensed occasionally the existence of parts of the planet which should, by all the laws he knew, be in the same space-time. But they were not— they existed *outside* in many other levels of the multiverse.

He continued to probe and at last found what he was searching for—sentient life. A warmth filled him momentarily.

Had he found the dwellers? These beings appeared not wholly solid, seemed to exist on *all* layers of the multiverse!

Could it be possible? he wondered. Did these beings exist on all planes and thus experience the full knowledge of reality, unlike the denizens who only saw their own particular universe and only experienced a fraction of the multiverse?

Though he could conceive the possibility, his mind could not imagine what these beings might be like, or what they saw. Perhaps he would find out?

He understood now why Mary the Maze played insanely with her lifeless keyboard in a tavern on Entropium.

Another thought came to him and he felt about with his mind and learned, with a sinking regret, that the Shaarn had succeeded in beating back the Thron. He could not tell definitely, but it seemed that the Shifter's motion through the multiversal levels was slowing down.

Hastily he re-located the dwellers. There were not many and they were on a part of the planet he felt he could find— a part not having its whole existence in the area now occupied by the Shifter, but probably visible to the human eye. With the aid of the conservator he felt fairly certain of finding the mysterious Hole.

Speed was important, but so was caution. He did not wish to suffer an ironical end—perishing now that he was so close to his goal.

He brought the ship down over a *gap* in order to test the conservator's powers.

They were extremely strong. As he came closer, the planet seemed to form itself under him as the missing piece shifted into place like a section of a jig-saw puzzle. It worked.

Now Renark lifted the ship away again and saw the piece fade back, wrenched into its previous continuum. He could not afford to land his ship on such a dangerous location. So he moved on and came down slowly on a surface which, he hoped, would remain in this continuum until he was ready to return.

If he did return, he told himself. The ominous activity near the binary was increasing, perhaps, already, the Shifter had stopped!

Asquiol was silent. He clutched the conservator to him as he followed Renark out of the ship's airlock.

The planet seemed a formless mass of swirling gases and they received a distinct sense of weightlessness for a moment as they placed their feet on its unnatural surface.

Dominated by the dreamlike insecurity of the planet, striking, first, patches of weightlessness, and later patches where their feet seemed entrenched in dragging mud, they moved warily on, Renark in the lead.

Though it was dark, the planet seemed to possess its own luminous aura, so that they could see a fair distance around them. But there were places where, somehow, their vision could not penetrate—yet they could see beyond these places! Even when they walked on rocky ground, it seemed impermanent.

As they moved, the area immediately around them would sometimes alter as the conservator exerted its strange power.

But, as if to compensate for this, new *gaps* continued to form elsewhere.

Struggling to keep his objective clear, Renark felt ahead with his mind, awed by the remarkable fluxions taking place constantly.

The planet was perpetually *shifting*. It was impossible to tell which part of it would be in existence even for a few moments at a time. Sundered matter, as chaotic as the unformed stuff of the multiverse at the dawn of creation, wrenched, spread and flung itself about as if in agony.

But, remorselessly, Renark pushed onward, filled with a sense of purpose which dominated his whole being.

Stumbling on, drunk by their visions of chaos, they did not lose their objective for a moment.

Sometimes near, sometimes distant, the Hole became their lode-star, beckoning them with a promise of truth—or destruction!

EIGHT

At last, after more than a weary day, they stood above the Hole, and as rock unformed itself and became gas, Renark said hollowly:

'They are in there. This is where we'll find them, but I do not know what they are.'

Though their tiredness made them inactive, Renark felt that he had never been more conscious, more receptive to what he saw. But his reception was passive. He could only look at the shifting, shining, dark and myriad-coloured Hole as it throbbed with power and energy.

They stared down at it, filled with knowledge and emotion. After several hours silence, Asquiol spoke.

'What now?' he said.

'This is the gateway of which we learned on Thron and Ekiversh,' said Renark. 'I can do nothing now but descend into it in the hope of achieving our aim.' Now the human race seemed remote, a fantasy, unreal—and yet important. More important than it had ever been before.

He moved towards the very brink of the Hole and lowered himself into its pulsing embrace.

Asquiol paused for a moment behind him and then followed. They ceased to climb down, for they were now floating, going neither up nor down, nor in any definite direction, but yet floating—somewhere. The conservator had ceased to work—unless it still worked and, in some way, these laws applied more rigorously to it than any it had previously conserved.

Again they were on solid ground, on a small island in an ocean. They stepped forward and knew they were in the heart of a blazing sun; stepped back and were in the middle of a bleak mountain range. From the tops of the mountains an entity looked down and welcomed them.

They moved towards it and were suddenly in an artificial chamber which seemed, at first, to have dead, black walls. Then they realised they were looking out into a void—emptiness.

To their left a being appeared.

It seemed to be constantly fading and reappearing. Like a badly-tuned laser set, Renark thought, desperately looking for something to cling to. He felt cut off entirely from anything he knew.

The being began to speak. It was not Terran he spoke. He conversed in a combination of sonic and thoughtwaves which struck responses in Renark's mind and body. He realised that these entities may have once been like himself, but had lost the power of direct speech when they gained the power to dwell on all levels of the multiverse.

He found he could communicate with the entity by modulating his own speech and thinking as far as possible in pictures.

'*You wish* (complicated geometric patterns) *help* . . .?'

'Yes (picture of universe contracting) . . .'

'*You from* (picture of a pregnant woman which changed quickly to a womb—an embryo, not quite human, appeared in it) . . .?'

Renark deliberated the meaning of this, but did not take long to realise what the entity was trying to say. Already he had half realised the significance.

Logic, based on the evidence he had seen and heard in the rest of the Shifter, was leading Renark towards an inescapable conclusion.

'Yes,' he said.

'*You must wait.*'

78

'For what?'

'Picture of a vast universe, multi-planed, turning about a central point. *Until* (picture of the Shifter moving through time, space and other dimensions towards the Hub).'

Renark realised what the picture meant. It could only mean one thing. He had only been shown it briefly, yet he understood clearly.

He had been snown the centre of the universe, the original place through which all the universal radii passed, from which all things had come. There were no alternate universes at the centre. When the Shifter passed through the centre—what . . .?

But what if the Shaarn succeeded in stopping the system's progress before it reached the Hub? He had to dismiss the idea. If the Shifter stopped too soon there would be no need for further speculation. No need for anything.

'What will happen there (misty picture of the multiverse)?' he asked.

'*Truth. You must wait here until* (Hub with Shifter) *then go* (the binary star—the Shifter's star) . . .'

He had to wait in Limbo until the Shifter reached the Hub and then they must journey towards—no, *into*—the sun!

He transmitted a horrified picture of himself and Asquiol burning.

The being said : '*No,*' and disappeared again.

When it reappeared, Renark said : 'Why?'

'You are expected.' The being faded, then vanished.

Since time did not exist here they couldn't tell how long they had waited. There were none of the usual bodily indications that time was passing.

Quite simply, they were in Limbo.

Every so often the being, or one like it, would reappear. Sometimes he would impart information regarding the Shifter's slow progress, sometimes he would just be there. Once a number of his kind appeared but vanished immediately.

Then, finally, the dweller appeared and a picture of the Shifter entering the area of the Multiversal Centre manifested itself in Renark's mind.

With relief and a bounding sense of anticipation, he prepared to experience—*Truth*.

Soon, whether he lived or died, remained sane or went insane, he would know. He and Asquiol would be the first of their race to *know*.

And this, they both realised, was all that mattered.

Then they went outwards.

They went towards the flaring, agonisingly brilliant suns.

They felt they had no physical form as they had known it, and yet could sense the stuff of their bodies clinging about them.

They poured their massless bodies into the fiery heat, the heart of the star, and eventually came to the Place of the Originators—not their natural habitat, but a compromise between Renark's and theirs.

They saw, without using their eyes, the Originators.

They could hear the Originators communicating, but there was no sound. All was colour, light and formlessness. Yet everything had a quality of bright existence, true reality.

'You are here,' said the Originators musingly, as one. 'We have been awaiting you and grown somewhat impatient. Your rate of development was not what we had hoped.'

On behalf of his race, in the knowledge of what the Originators meant, Renark said: 'I am sorry.'

'You were always a race to progress only when danger threatened.'

'Do we still exist?' Renark asked.

'Yes.'

'For how long?' Asquiol spoke for the first time.

The Originators did not answer his question directly. Instead, they said:

'You wish us to make changes. We expected this. That is why we speeded up the metamorphosis of your universe. You understand that although your universe is contracting, it will still exist as individual galaxies, suns and planets, matter of most kinds in different formations?'

'But the human race—what of that?'

'We should have let it die. Intelligent organic life cannot undergo the strains of the change. If you had not come to us, we should have let it die—regretfully. But our judgment was correct. We let you know of the coming catastrophe and you used all your resources of will and judgment to come here as we hoped you would.'

There was a pause, and then the Originators continued:

'Like all other races in the multiverse, yours is capable of existing on all levels. Not just one. But, because of these links you have with the rest of the levels, you would have perished, being not fully natural to just one level. None of the intelligent forms could survive such a catastrophe. We were responsible for placing them all in their present environment. Each plane of the multiverse serves as a separate seeding bed for a multitude of races, one of which may survive and succeed us. Your plane serves, in your terms, as a womb. You are our children—our hope. But if you fail to overcome the special limitations we set upon you, you, like us, shall die. But you shall die . . . still-born.'

'Then what is to become of us?'

'We made the changes in your universe in order to accelerate your rate of development, so that representatives of your race would find a way to us. To the greatest extent you have succeeded, but you must return rapidly and inform your race of their need to develop more rapidly, more dynamically. We shall afford you the means, this time, of evacuating your universe. But we are growing old, and you, of all the intelligent races in the multiverse, are needed to take our place. You cannot do that until you are ready. Either you succeed in achieving your birthright, or, like us, perish in chaos and agony.

'You have proved to us that we were justified in selecting you, but you *can* overcome the boundaries we set around you. But hurry, we beg you—hurry . . .'

'What will happen if we succeed?'

'You will experience a stage of metamorphosis. Soon you will no longer need a universe of the kind you know now. Things are coming to an end. You have the choice of life— more than life or death!'

Renark accepted this. It was all he could do.

'And us—what is our function now?'

'To perform what you set out to do.'

There was a long, long pause.

Womb-warmth filled the two men and time stopped for them as the Originators exuded sympathy and understanding. But glowing like hard reality beneath this, Renark sensed— his own oblivion? His own death? Something lay there in the future. Something ominous was in store for him.

'You are right, Renark,' said the Originators.

'I can't be right or wrong. I have no idea what my fate is.'

'But you sense, perhaps, our foreknowledge of your termination as a physical entity—perhaps your end as a conscious entity. It is hard to tell. Your spirit is a great one, Renark—a mighty spirit that is too great for the flesh that chains it. It must be allowed to spread, to permeate the multiverse!'

'So be it,' Renark said slowly.

Asquiol could neither understand nor believe what the Originators were saying. His form—golden, flashing red—bounced and flared before Renark as he said:

'Are you to die, Renark?'

'No! No!'

Renark's voice roared like a tower of flame. He addressed his friend. 'When I am gone you must lead our race. You must direct them towards their destiny—or perish with them. Do you understand?'

'I accept what you say, but without understanding. This experience is driving us to madness!'

The cool tones of the Originators swept inwards like flowing ice to catch their attention and silence them.

'Not yet, not yet. You must both retain something of your old forms and your old convictions. Your part is not played out yet. Now that you understand the nature of the multiverse, it will not be difficult to supply you with material means for escaping your shrinking universe. We will give you knowledge of a machine to produce a warp effect and enable your people to travel to another, safer universe where they will undergo further tests. Our plans have not fully worked themselves out yet. There are others of your race involved—and you must meet and react and harden one another before you can fulfill the destiny we offer you. You, Asquiol, will be entrusted with this part of the mission.'

'Renark is the strongest,' Asquiol said quietly.

'Therefore Renark's spirit must be sacrificed as a gift to the rest of you. This is necessary.'

'How shall we accomplish this exodus to a new universe?' Renark asked hollowly.

'We will help. We shall instil in your fellow creatures a trust in the word of you both. It will necessarily be a temporary thing. Once you have left your universe, our workings must be of a subtler sort, and only the efforts of certain individuals will save you.'

'We shall be on our own?' Asquiol questioned.

'Virtually, yes.'

'What shall we find in this new universe?'

'We do not know, for it is likely that your jump will be a random one into *any* of the other multiversal planes. We cannot guarantee you a friendly reception. There are forces opposed to our purpose—meaner intellects who strive to prevent the evolution of our being.'

'Our being?' Asquiol's shape flickered and re-formed.

'Yours—ours—everyone's. We, the Originators, call ourselves Intelligent Optimists, since we see a purpose, of sorts, to existence. But there are pessimists in the universe. They prey upon us, seek to destroy us, since they themselves have given up hope of ever breaking the bonds which chain them to the half-real state in which they exist. They have their unknowing supporters among your own segment of the total race.'

'I understand.'

With those two words they became whole men. They saw, at last, the real universe—the myriad-planed universe comprising many, many dimensions so that there was no empty space at all, but a crowded, rich existence through which they had previously moved unknowing.

With an effort of his titanic will, Renark said urgently: 'One thing. What *is* your purpose? What is our ultimate purpose?'

'To exist,' was the simple reply. 'You cannot have, as yet, real knowledge of what that means. Existence is the beginning and the end. Whatever significance you choose to put upon it is irrelevant. If we were to die before you were ready to take our place, then all our creation would die. The multiverse would die. Chaos would flood over everything and a formless, mindless, fluctuating shroud would mark our passing.'

'We do not want that,' said Asquiol and Renark together.

'Neither do we. That is why you are here. Now—the information you will need.'

Their minds, it seemed, were taken by a gentle hand and sent along a certain course of logic until, at length, they had complete understanding of the principle involved in building dimension-travelling space-ships.

In what was, for them, normal space-time, it would have been virtually impossible to have formulated the principle in all its aspects. But now, dwelling in the whole multiverse, the logic seemed simple. They were confident that they could impart the information to their own race.

'Are you satisfied?' the Originators asked.

'Perfectly,' Renark said. 'We must hurry now, and return to our own universe. The exodus must begin as soon as possible.'

'Farewell, Renark. It is unlikely that when we meet again you will remember us. Farewell, Asquiol. When *we* meet again let us hope that you have succeeded in this matter.'

'Let us hope so,' Asquiol said gravely.

Then their beings were spreading backwards and streaming through the multiverse towards the ship which still lay on Roth.

NINE

The traveller stopped at the sagging filling station, the last human artifact before the long, grey road began again.

A huge, shapeless haversack bulged on his stooping back, but he walked along effortlessly, smiling in the depths of his lean, black face, his hair and beard wild about him.

Kaal Yinsen whistled to himself and took the road North. It was several centuries since the Earth had been populated by more than the few thousand people living here now, and this was the way he liked it. Kaal Yinsen had never had a dream in his life, and when this one came it came with force.

The road faded, the whole surface of the planet reared up, whirled and bellowed. Suddenly he knew he must head South again. This he did and was joined, on the way, by hundreds of families going in the same direction.

Bossan Glinqvist, Lord of Orion, sat in an office which was part of an isolated metal city, hanging in space close to the heart of the galaxy. He picked up the file on Drenner Macneer and began to leaf through it, not sure that his duties as Moderator in the Council of Galactic Lords were sufficiently satisfying to make him live a third of his adult life in so unnatural an environment. Macneer's case was a difficult one, requiring all Glinqvist's concentration and intelligence to judge.

The man had instigated a breach-of-code suit against the Council—accusing it of failing to represent the interests of a minority group of traders who, because of a change in a tariff agreement between Lanring and Balesorn in the Clive System, had lost their initiative to survive by labour and were currently living off the citizen's grant on a remote outworld. It was a serious matter. Glinqvist looked up, frowning, and experienced a powerful hallucination.

Soon afterwards he was giving orders for the city to be set in motion—an unprecedented order—and directed toward the Kassim System.

These were but two examples of what was happening to every intelligent denizen of the galaxy.

Every human being, adult or child, was filled with the same compulsion to journey towards certain central planets where they gathered—and waited patiently.

On Earth, the few inhabitants of the planet felt that the very ground would give beneath the weight of so many new-comers. Normally, they would have been resentful of the appearance of outsiders on the recently healed globe, but now, with them, they waited.

And at last they were rewarded.

They saw its vague outlines in the sky. On laser screens all over the planet they watched it land on a tendril of fire. A spaceship—a Police cruiser. It was scarred and battered. It looked old and scarcely spaceworthy.

There was silence everywhere as they watched the airlock open and two figures emerge.

Millions of pairs of eyes winced and failed to focus properly upon the figures. They strained to see *all* the figures, but it was impossible. The men who came out of the ship were like ghostly chameleons, their hazy bodies shifting with colour and energy and light.

The watchers seemed to see many images overlaid on the two they recognised as men, images which seemed to stretch out into other dimensions beyond their powers to see or to imagine.

These visitors were like angels. Their set faces glowed with knowledge; the matter of their bodies was iridescent; their words, when they began to speak, throbbed in tempo with the pulse of the planet so that it was as if they heard an earthquake speak, or an ocean or a volcano, or even the sun itself giving voice!

Yet they understood that these messengers were human. But humans so altered that it was almost impossible to regard them as such.

They listened in awe to the words and, in part at least, they understood what they must do.

Renark and Asquiol delivered the ultimate message. They told of the threat inherent in the contracting universe. They told how this had come about and why. And then they told how the destruction of the race could be avoided.

They spoke clearly, in careful terms, looking out at their listeners from the depths of their faraway minds. No longer existing wholly in any one plane of the multiverse, they needed to concentrate in order to keep this single level in complete focus.

The myriad dimensions of the multiverse coursed in ever-changing beauty as they spoke. But this experience they could not as yet convey, for it was beyond speech. And the stuff of their bodies changed with the multiverse in scintillating harmony so that the watchers could not always see them as men. But, nonetheless, they listened.

They listened and learned that the multiverse contained many levels and that their universe was but one level—a fragment of the great whole. That it was finite, yet beyond the power of their minds to comprehend. They learned that this structure had been created by beings called the Originators. They learned that the Originators, sensing they would die, had created the multiverse as a seeding ground for a race to take their place. They learned that they, the embryonic children of the Originators, were to be given their last chance to take over. They were given a choice: Understand and overcome the pseudo-real boundaries of time and space as they understood them, therefore claiming their birthright— or perish!

Then Renark and Asquiol left the planet Earth, passing on to another and then another to impart their news.

Wherever they passed they left behind them awed silence, and each human being that heard them was left with a feeling of *completeness* such as he knew he had been searching for all his life.

Then the two multi-faceted messengers called technicians and scientists and philosophers to them and told these men what they must do.

Soon after, the vehicles, which had been fitted with the Intercontinua-travelling device, swarmed in the depths of space beyond the Rim, ready to carry the human race into another universe.

At the head of the tremendous space-caravan the small, battered Police cruiser lay. In it, Renark and Asquiol took their final leave of one another.

Outside the cruiser, a small space-car awaited Renark.

The two beings—the New Men—looked at one another's shifting forms, stared about them to absorb the pulsating sight of the total multiverse, clasped hands, but said nothing. It was pre-ordained that this must happen.

Sorrowfully, Asquiol watched his friend board the space-car and vanish back towards the Hub of the galaxy.

Now he had to make ready the giant fleet. The Galactic Lords had sworn him full powers of leadership until such a time as he would no longer be needed. The efficient administration which had run the galaxy for many years was admirably suited to organising the vast fleet and they took Asquiol's orders and translated them into action.

'At precisely 1800 hours General Time, each ship will engage its I.T. drive.' Asquiol's lonely voice echoed across the void through which the fleet drifted.

Somewhere, out of sight of Asquiol or the human race, a small figure halted its space-car, climbed into a suit, clambered from the car and hung in space as it drifted away.

Now they could observe the galaxies rushing down upon one another. They came together and joined in one blazing symphony of light as the human race plunged through the dimensions to the safety of another universe where another intelligent life-form waited to receive it—perhaps in friendship, perhaps in resentment.

Then the contraction was swifter, sudden.

And Renark remained behind. Why, the race would never know—and even Renark was uncertain of his reasons. He only knew there had to be a sacrifice. Was it the ancient creed of his savage ancestors, translated into the terms of the Originators? Or did his action have some greater meaning? There would be no answer. There could be none.

Faster and faster, the universe contracted until all of it existed in an area that seemed little larger than Renark's hand. Still it shrank, as Renark watched it now as if from a distance. Then it vanished from his sight, though he could still sense it, was still aware of its rapidly decreasing size.

He knew that there was a point to which a thing can be reduced before it ceases to exist, and finally that point was reached. Now there was a gap, a real flaw in the fabric of the multiverse itself. His universe, the galaxy, the Earth, were no longer there—possibly absorbed into a larger universe beyond even Renark's marvellous senses. Perhaps, in this greater universe, his universe existed as a photon somewhere. Only Renark was left, his shifting, shimmering body moving in a void, the stuff of it beginning to dissipate and disappear.

'God!' he said as everything vanished.

His voice echoed and ached through the deserted gulf and Renark lived that moment for ever.

TEN

In his deep sorrow, Asquiol was resolved to carry on Renark's work and bring to finality the Originators' plans for the human race.

The fleet was dropping, dropping, dropping through layer after layer of the multiverse in a barely controlled escape dive.

Soon he must give the order to slow down and halt on one level. He had no idea which to choose. Though he was aware of the multiverse, his vision, unlike Renark's, could not extend beyond its previous limits. He had no inkling of what to expect in the universe in which they would finally stop.

In the great multiverse they were merely a scattering of seeds—seeds that must survive many elements if they were to grow.

Finite, yet containing the stuff of infinity, the multiverse wheeled in its gigantic movement through space.

To those who could observe it from beyond its boundaries —the Originators—it appeared as a solid construction, dense and huge. Yet within it there were many things, many intelligences who did not realise that they dwelt in the multiverse, since each layer was separated from another by dimensions. Dimensions that were like leaves between the layers.

Here and there the mighty structure was flawed—by fragments which moved *through* the dimensions, through the leaves, passing many universes; by a vacuum existing where one small part had vanished. But, on the whole, the universes remained unknown to one another. They did not realise that they were part of a composite structure of fantastic complexity. They did not realise their purpose or the purpose for which the multiverse had been created.

Only the chosen knew—and of them only a few understood.

So, fleeing from their new non-existent galaxy, the human race began its great exodus into a new space-time-continuum —pierced the walls of the dimension-barrier and came, at last, into a new universe.

By this action, Man had also entered a new period of his history.

But Asquiol of Pompeii was no longer a man. He had become many men and was therefore complete. Now there was no better leader for the human fleet; no better mentor to guide it. For Asquiol was the New man. Existing in a multitude of dimensions, his vision extended beyond the limitations of his fellows, and saw all that men could one day become—if they could make the effort.

Asquiol of Pompeii, captain of destiny, destroyer of boundaries, becalmed in detachment, opened his eyes from a sad reverie and observed the fleet he led.

His screen showed him the vast caravan of vessels. There were space-liners and battleships, launches and factory-ships, ships of all kinds and for all purposes, containing all the machinery of a complex society on the move. There were ships of many designs, some ornate, some plain, containing one part in common—the I.T. drive.

Asquiol deliberately ceased to wonder why Renark had elected to stay behind in the dying universe. But he still wished it had not happened. He missed the confidence which had come to him from Renark's presence, from Renark's will and spirit. But Renark and his will were in the past now. Asquiol had to find strength only from within himself—or perish.

And if he perished, ceased to be what he was, then the danger of the race itself perishing would be heightened considerably. Therefore, he reasoned, his survival and the survival of the race were linked.

Twenty-four hours of relative time had not passed since the fleet left the home universe. He decided that the next universe, irrespective of what it was, should be the one to remain in. Quickly he gave the order.

'De-activate I.T. drive at 1800 hours.'

At 1800 hours exactly, the fleet ceased to fall through the dimensions and found itself entering the fringes of a strange galaxy, not knowing what they might encounter or what danger might exist here.

On board the administration ships, men worked on data which was pouring in.

They charted the galaxy; they learned that, in construction, it was scarcely different from their own. Asquiol wasn't surprised—each layer of the multiverse differed only slightly from the next.

Guide Sensers investigated the nearer suns and planets, while telepaths explored the widespread systems for signs of intelligent life. If they discovered such life they would then have to assess, if possible, its attitude towards the refugee-invaders now entering the confines of its galaxy. This was a new technique. One which Asquiol had learned from the Shaarn.

Flanking the fleet were the great battlewagons of the Galactic Police, now entrusted with the guardianship of the mighty caravan as it plunged at fantastic speed through the scattering of suns that was the Rim of the spiral galaxy.

Hazy lights filled space for several miles in all directions, the ships of the fleet swimming darkly through it. Beyond the fleet was the sharper darkness and beyond that the faint sparks of the stars. The light emanated from the ships like a swirling, intangible nebula, moving constantly towards a destination it might never reach.

But Asquiol saw more than this. For Asquiol saw the multiverse.

It required, in fact, a certain effort now to devote his attention to only one plane, no matter how vast. As soon as he relaxed his attention, he felt the absolute pleasure of dwelling on all the planes simultaneously, of seeing around him all that there was in the area of the multiverse he now occupied.

It was like existing in a place where the very air was jewelled and faceted, glistening and alive with myriad colours, flashing, scintillating, swirling and beautiful.

This was a richer thing, the multiverse as a whole. In it Asquiol could see his own fleet and the faraway stars, but the space between everything was crammed full. The multiverse was packed thick with life and matter. There was not an inch which did not possess something of interest. Vacuum

90

was, in a sense, that which separated one layer from another. When all the layers were experienced as a whole, there was no wasted vacuum, no dark nothingness. Here was everything at once, all possibilities, all experience.

He was suddenly forced to pull himself back from this individual experience. The special alarm over his laser-screen was shrilling urgently.

A face appeared on the screen. It was pouched and puffy, heavily jowelled like that of a bloodhound.

'Lord Mordan,' Asquiol said to the Galactic Lord who was Captain-in-chief of Police.

'Asquiol.' Even now Asquiol's power was virtually absolute, Mordan couldn't bring himself to call him "prince," for the Galactic Council had not had time to restore the now meaningless title. Mordan spoke heavily:

'Our Guide Sensers and Mind Sensers have come up with important information. We have located and contacted an intelligent species who appear to have noticed our entry into this space-time. They are evidently a star-travelling race.'

'How have they reacted to our entry?'

'We aren't sure—the sensers are finding it difficult to adjust to their minds . . .'

'Naturally, it will take time to understand a non-human species. Let me know if you have any further news.'

Mordan had been screwing up his eyes while looking at Asquiol's image. There appeared to be several images, in fact, each containing a different combination of colours, overlapping one another. It was as if Asquiol looked out at Mordan through a series of tinted, opaque masks covering his body and interleaving on either side. The image that Mordan took to be the original lay slightly to one side of the multiple image and, for him, in better focus than the rest. He evidently could not equate this image with what he remembered—the cynical, moody, vital young man whom he had divested of title and power years before. Now he saw a lean, saturnine man, the face that of a fallen archangel, stern with the weight of leadership, the eyes sharp yet staring into a distance containing little that Mordan felt he could observe.

With his usual feeling of relief, Mordan switched out and relayed Asquiol's message to the senser team.

As he waited for further news, Asquiol didn't exert his mind by trying to contact the new species directly.

That would come later. He decided to allow the sensers

time to assemble as much general data as possible before he turned his full attention to the problem.

He kept in mind the Originators' warning that certain intelligences were quite likely to receive the human race with insensate hostility, but he hoped the universe they were in contained life that would welcome them and allow them to settle where they could. If the intelligences were hostile, the fleet was equipped to fight—and, in the last resort, run. He had already ordered the lifting of the ban on the anti-neutron cannon, and this devastating armament was virtually invincible. As far as he knew there was no known screen that could withstand it. The fleet was already alerted for battle. There was nothing to do at the moment but wait and see.

He returned his thoughts to problems of a different nature.

Landing on and settling new planets within this galaxy would only be a minor problem compared with the task of taking over from the Originators.

He thought of his race as a chicken in an egg. Within the shell it was alive, but aware of nothing beyond the shell, but with the act of breaking through the barrier of dimensions separating its universe from others, it had broken from its enclosing and stifling shell to some awareness of the multiverse and the exact nature of things.

But a hatched chicken, thought Asquiol, may believe the breaking of the shell to be the ultimate action of its life—until the shell shattered and the whole world was visible in all its complexity. Then it discovered the farmyard and the countryside with all their many dangers. It discovered that it was only a chick and must learn and act to survive if it was to grow to adulthood.

And what, Asquiol considered ironically, was the eventual fate of the average chicken? He wondered how many other races had got this far in the ages of the multiverse's existence. Only one would survive, and now it had to be the human race, for if it did not attain its birthright before the Originators died, then none would take its place. The multiverse would disintegrate back into the chaotic forces from which the Originators had formed it.

Death and the stuff of death would engulf the cosmos. The tides of chance would roll over all existing things, and the multiverse, bereft of guidance and control, would collapse.

All intelligence, as the Originators and their creations understood it, would perish!

It was this knowledge that enabled him to keep his objective in the forefront. The race must not perish; it must survive and progress, must achieve the marvellous birthright that was its promised destiny. The race must replace the Originators while there was still a little time.

Was there sufficient time?

Asquiol didn't know. He had no way of knowing when the Originators would die. He had, in this case, to attempt to pack centuries of evolution into the shortest possible period. Whether, immediate danger averted, the race would allow him to continue with his mission he did not know. Now that the weird influence of the Originators had been removed, mankind could throw away its birthright, and consequently the life of all ordered creation, by one ill-judged or fear-inspired decision.

Even now there were elements in the fleet who questioned his leadership, questioned his vision and his motives. It was easy to understand this questioning, suspicious impulse which was at once man's salvation and doom. Without it he ceased to reason; with it he often ceased to act. To *use* the impulse objectively was the answer. Asquiol knew. But how?

Without the usual warning, Mordan's face appeared on the laser. He stared into emptiness since he preferred not to have to see Asquiol's disturbing image.

'These intelligences are obviously preparing to attack us,' he said urgently.

So the worst had happened. In which case the threat must be met. 'What preparations are you making?' Asquiol said in a level voice.

'I have alerted our battle force and all essential craft are now protected by energy screens—administration ships, farm ships, factory ships. These I intend to reassemble at the centre of our formation since they are necessary for survival.

'Around these I will put all residential ships. The third section comprises all fighting craft, including privately owned vessels with worthwhile armament. The operation is working fairly smoothly, though there are a few recalcitrants I'm having difficulty with. We are forming to totally enclose your ship so that you are properly protected.'

Asquiol drew a deep breath and said slowly: 'Thank you,

93

Lord Mordan. That sounds most efficient.' To Mordan, his voice seemed to produce—like his image—intrinsic, faraway echoes that carried past Mordan and beyond him. 'How do you intend to deal with these recalcitrants?'

'I have conferred with the other members of the Galactic Council and we have come to a decision—subject to your approval.'

'That decision is?'

'We will have to use more direct powers of action—make emergency laws only to be declared null and void after the danger has passed.

'The example of history should deter you from such a decision. Powers of dictatorship, which you give me and yourselves, once assumed are liable to last beyond the circumstances for which they were devised. We have not employed coercion, force, or anything like it, for several centuries!'

'Asquiol—there is no time for debate!'

Asquiol made up his mind immediately. Survival, for the moment, was of primary importance. 'Very well. Take on these powers—force the recalcitrants to obey our orders, but be sure not to abuse the powers or we will find ourselves weakened rather than strengthened.'

'This we know. Thank you.'

Asquiol watched, his mood brooding and disquieted, as the fleet re-deployed into a great oval shape with his own battered ship in the centre, the nut in an inordinately thick shell.

ELEVEN

Adam Roffrey was a psychopath, a rebel without a cause, a hater of state and organisation.

Adam Roffrey morosely watched the ships re-forming about him, but remained where he was, refusing to answer the signal on his screen. His large head, made larger by the thick, black beard and hair covering it, had a dogged, insolent set. He was refusing to budge and he knew he was within his rights.

The flexible laws of the galaxy had been bent by him many times, for the rights of the citizen were varied and complex. He could not be forced to take part in a war; without his permission the authorities could not even contact him. Therefore, he sat tight, ignoring the urgent signal.

When Lord Mordan's bloodhound face appeared, unauthorised, on the laser-screen, Roffrey disguised his shock and smiled sardonically. He said lightly, as he always said things, whatever the gravity of the statement:

'It's a lost cause, Lord Mordan. We can't hope to win. We must be fantastically outnumbered. Asquiol's forcing the race to commit suicide. Are we voting?'

'No,' said Mordan, 'we're not. For the duration of the emergency all citizen's rights are liable to be waived if necessary. You have no choice but to comply with the decision of Asquiol and the Galactic Council. Asquiol knows what's best.'

'He doesn't know what's best for me. I'm the only lost cause I've ever backed, and that's the way it's staying!'

Lord Mordan regarded the black-bearded giant grinning out of the laser screen and he frowned.

'Nobody leaves the fleet, Roffrey. For one thing, it's too dangerous, and for another we've got to keep it tight and organised if we're to survive!'

He said the last words to a blank screen. He whirled round in his control chair and shouted to a passing captain.

'Alert the perimiter guard. A ship may try to leave. Stop it!'

'How, Lord Mordan?'

'Force—if there is no other alternative,' said Mordan, shocking the captain, who had never received such an order in his whole career.

Adam Roffrey had been anti-social all his life.

His living had been made on the fringes of the law. He wasn't going to give in to the demands of society now. The chips were down for the fleet—that was his guess—and he had no reason for sticking around. He objected to the discipline required to fight complicated space-battles; he objected to the odds against the human race winning the battles; he objected to the fact that he was being personally involved. Personal involvement was not in his line.

So he broke the energy seals on his anti-neutron cannon and prepared to blast out. As he moved away from the rest of the fleet, several Geepee gunboats, alerted by Mordan, flitted towards him from nadir-north-west.

95

He rubbed his hairy chin, scratched his hairy forehead and reached out a hairy hand to his drive control. At full power he retreated, away from the oncoming ships, away from the fleet, into the unknown space of the unknown universe.

He was prepared to take such chances to avoid curtailment of his personal liberty.

But his ship, a peculiar vessel, at first sight an impossible old hulk, a space launch got up to look like a merchantman and fitted like a battle-wagon, could not hope to outdistance the Geepee craft in the long run. Already they were beginning to catch up.

Humming to himself, he debated his best course of action.

There was one sure method of evading immediate danger as well as the alien threat already visible as a huge fleet of spherical vessels, seen on his screens, approached the fleet from the depths of space.

But to take that way out, although he had considered it much earlier in another context, could be highly dangerous.

The odds were that, if he committed himself to it, he would never see another human being again.

The necessity to make a decision was increasing.

His ship, like all those in the great cosmic caravan, was fitted with the I.T. drive enabling him to travel through the dimensions. He had already taken the trouble to learn all he could about multi-dimensional space and certain things existing in it. He knew, suddenly, where he was going.

The idea had been in the back of his mind for years. Now he would be forced to go.

The Geepee ships were getting closer, their warning blaring on his communicator. He pressed a button of his chart-viewer, keeping a wary eye on the oncoming ships.

Though the Geepees were nearer, the two embattled fleets were far behind. He saw faint splashes of coloured light on his screen. He was tense and was surprised to note that he had a feeling half of relief, half of guilt that he had missed the battle. He wasn't a coward, but now he had something to do.

A quick glance at the slide of equations on the viewer and his hand was reaching for the crudely constructed controls of the I.T. drive. He pulled a lever, adjusted the controls, and quite suddenly the Geepee ships seemed to fade away. And fading into the place where they had been was a backdrop of great blazing suns that made his eyes ache.

Once again he experienced the unique sensation of falling through the layers of the multiverse.

Rapidly, as he operated the I.T. drive, the suns faded to be replaced by cold vacuum, which was replaced by an agitation of gases heaving about in an unformed state, scarlet and grey. He was phasing quickly through the layers, through universe after universe with only a slight feeling of nausea in his stomach and a fierce determination to reach his destination.

The Geepee ships hadn't followed him.

They had probably decided that their first priority was to aid the human fleet.

He travelled through space as well as time and the separating dimensions, and he was heading back in the direction where in his home universe, the edge of the galaxy had been. He had all the bearings he needed and, as he moved on one level, he moved through others at reckless speed.

He knew where he was going—but whether he would make it was a question he couldn't answer.

Asquiol of Pompeii watched the battle on his screens with a feeling akin to helplessness. Mordan was conducting the war, needing only basic orders from him.

Am I doing as much as I could? he wondered. Am I not accepting too complacently, what I have discovered?

It was easy for him to dominate the fleet, for his mind had become at once flexible and strong and his physical presence overawed his fellows. There was a part of him, too, which was not at ease, as if he were a jig-saw complete but for the last piece, and the section that would complete him was just—tantalisingly—out of reach.

Somewhere in the multiverse he felt the piece existed—perhaps another intelligence that he could share his thoughts and experiences with. He was almost certain it was out there, yet what it was and how he would find it he did not know. Without it, his picture of himself was incomplete. He felt that he functioned but could not progress. Had the Originators deliberately done this to him? Or had they made a mistake?

At first he had thought it was the loss of Renark which

gave him the sense of incompleteness. But Renark's loss was still there, inside him, kept out of mind as much as possible. No, this was another lack. A lack of what, though?

He bent closer to observe the battle.

The fleet's formation was lost as yet another wave of attackers pounced out of space with weapons cutting lances of bright energy.

They were not impervious to anti-neutron cannon, but the two forces were fairly matched as far as technology went. There were more of the aliens and they had the double advantage of being in home territory and defending it. This was what primarily worried Asquiol.

But he could do nothing decisive at the moment. He would have to wait.

Again, while Mordan sweated to withstand and retaliate against this fresh attack, Asquiol let his mind and being drop through the layers of the multiverse and contact the alien commanders. If they would not accept peace terms, he strove to arrange a truce.

To his surprise, this suggestion seemed acceptable to them.

There *was* an alternative to open war—one which they would be delighted to negotiate.

That was?

The Game, they said. Play the game with us—winner takes all.

After he had got some inkling of the Game's nature, Asquiol deliberated momentarily. There were pros and cons . . .

Finally, he agreed and was soon watching the enemy ships retreating away into the void.

With some trepidation, he informed Mordan of his decision and awaited its outcome.

This new development in their struggle with the aliens disturbed Lord Mordan. War he could understand. This, at first, he could not. All psychologists, psychiatrists, physiologists and kindred professionals had been ordered to the huge factory ship which engineers were already converting.

From now on, according to Asquiol, the battle was to be fought from this single ship—and it had no armaments!

Asquiol was unapproachable as he conferred with the alien commanders in his own peculiar way. Every so often he would break off to issue strange orders.

Something about a game. Yet what kind of game, wondered Lord Mordan, required experts in psychology as its players? What was the complicated electronic equipment that technicians were installing in the great converted hold of the factory ship?

'This is our only chance of winning,' Asquiol had told him. 'A slim one—but if we learn how to play it properly, we have a chance.'

Mordan sighed. At least the truce had allowed them time to regroup and assess damage. The damage had been great. Two-thirds of the fleet had been destroyed. Farm ships and factory ships were working at full capacity to supply the fleet with necessities. But tight rationing had been introduced. The race was subsisting on survival rations. The initial joy of escape was replaced by gloomy desperation.

Adam Roffrey could see his destination.

He slammed the I.T. activator to the 'of' position and coasted towards the looming system ahead.

It hung in empty space, the outlines of its planets hazy, following a random progression around a magnificent binary sun.

The legendary system rose larger on his laser screen. The unnatural collection of worlds came closer.

The epic story of Renark and Asquiol on their quest to the Sundered Worlds was common lore among the human race these days. But the story—or, at least, part of it had had a special significance for Roffrey.

Renark and Asquiol had left two members of their party behind—Willow Kovacs and Paul Talfryn.

Roffrey knew their names. But dominant in his skull was another name—a woman's, the woman he had come to find.

If he did not find her this time, he told himself, then he would have to accept that she was dead. Then he would have to accept his own death also.

Such was the intensity of his obsession.

As he neared the Sundered Worlds he regarded them with curiosity. They had changed. The planets were spaced normally—not equidistantly, as he had thought. And, as far as he could tell, the system had stopped shifting.

Now he remembered part of the story which was fast becoming a myth among those who had fled their own galaxy. A dog-like race called the Shaarn had attempted to stop the system's course through the dimensions.

Evidently they'd succeeded.

His maps aided him to find Entropium and he cruised into the Shifter's area warily, for he knew enough to expect two kinds of danger—the Thron and the lawless nature of the Shifter itself.

Yet, wary as he was, it was impossible to observe either chaos or enemy as he swept down over Entropium, scanning the planet for the only city that had ever been built there.

He didn't find the city, either.

He found, instead, a place where a city had been. Now it was jagged rubble. He landed his ship on a scattered wasteland of twisted steel and smashed concrete.

Scanning the surrounding ruins, he saw shadowy shapes scuttling through the dark craters and between the shattered buildings. His experience told him nothing about the cause of this catastrophe.

At length, sick at heart, he climbed into space armour, strapped an anti-neutron pistol to his side, descended to the airlock and placed his booted feet on the planet's surface.

A bolt of energy flashed from a crater and spread itself over his force-screen. He staggered back to lean against one of his ship's landing fins, lugging the pistol from its holster.

He did not fire immediately for, like everyone else, he had a certain fear of the destructive effects of the a-n gun.

He saw an alien figure—a dazzling white skin like melted plastic covering a squat skeleton, long legs and short arms, but no head that he could see—appear over the edge of the crater, a long metal tube cradled in its arms and pointing at him.

He fired.

The thing's wailing shriek resounded in his helmet. It absorbed the buzzing stream of anti-neutrons, collapsed, melted and vanished.

'Over here!'

Roffrey turned to see a human figure, all rags and filth, waving to him. He ran towards it.

In a crater which had been turned into a crude fortress by the piles of wreckage surrounding its perimeter, Roffrey found a handful of wretches, the remnants of the human population of Entropium.

The man who had waved had a fleshless head and huge eyes. Dirty, scab-covered skin was drawn tight over his skull. He fingered his emaciated body and eyed Roffrey warily. He said:

'We're starving here. Have you got any supplies?'

'What happened?' Roffrey said, feeling sick.

There was desolation everywhere. These human beings had evidently banded together for protection against similar bands of aliens. Evidently, also, only the fittest survived.

The ragged man pointed at the rubble behind him. 'This? We don't know. It just hit us . . .'

'Why didn't you leave here?'

'No ships. Most of them were destroyed.'

Roffrey grimaced and said: 'Keep me covered while I return to my ship. I'll be back.'

A short time later he came stumbling back over the rubble with a box in his hands, his boots slipping and sliding on the uneven ground. They clustered around him greedily as he handed out vitapacks.

Something terrible had happened to the planet—perhaps to the whole system. He had to know what—and why.

Now a woman separated herself from the group squatting over their food. The man with the fleshless head followed her.

She said to Roffrey: 'You must be from the home galaxy. How did you get here?—Did they . . . find how the Shifter worked?'

'You mean Renark and Asquiol?'

Roffrey looked hard at the woman, but he didn't know her. He noted that she had obviously been beautiful, probably still was under the filth and rags. 'They got through. They discovered more than they bargained for here—but they got through. Our whole universe doesn't exist any more. But the race—or the part which left—is still going. Maybe it's wiped out by now. I don't know.'

The man with the fleshless head put his arm around the woman. They looked like a pair of animated skeletons and the man's action enhanced the bizarre effect.

'He didn't want you then and he won't now,' he said to her.

Roffrey saw tension between them, but couldn't understand why.

She said: 'Shut up, Paul. Are Renark and Asquiol safe?'

Roffrey shook his head. 'Renark's dead. Asquiol's okay— he's leading the fleet. The Gee-lord gave him complete leadership during the emergency. They work under him now.'

'Local boy makes good,' said the male skeleton.

Roffrey felt he could name both of them now. He pointed at the man. 'Are you Paul Talfryn?'

Talfryn nodded. He cocked his head towards the woman. She dropped her eyes. 'This is Willow Kovacs—my wife. We sort of got married . . . Asquiol's mentioned us, eh?. I suppose he sent you back for us?'

'No.'

Willow Kovacs shuddered. Roffrey reflected that she didn't appear to like Talfryn very much; there was a kind of apathetic hatred in her eyes. Probably she regarded Talfryn merely as a protector, even if that. But it was no business of his.

'What happened to the rest of the human population?' Roffrey said, concentrating on his own affairs and trying to ignore the sickening feeling of disgust at the sight of such degeneration. 'Were they all killed?'

'Did you see anything when you came through the ruins?' Talfryn asked. 'Little, scuttling animal shapes, maybe?'

Roffrey had seen them. They had been repulsive, though he didn't know why.

Talfryn said: 'All those little creatures were intelligent once. For some reason, the Shifter stopped shifting. There was a long period of absolute madness before she seemed to settle down again. This happened—that happened.

'When the trouble started, the actual forms of human beings and aliens changed, devolving into these. Somebody said it was metabolic pressures combined with time-slips induced by the stop, but I didn't understand it. I'm no scientist—an astro-geographer. Unlicensed, you know . . .' He seemed to sink into an attitude of detachment and then looked up suddenly. 'The city just crumbled. It was horrifying. A lot of people went mad. I suppose Asquiol told you . . .'

'I've never met Asquiol,' Roffrey broke in. 'All my information is second-hand. I came particularly to find another person. A woman—she helped Renark with information. Mary the Maze—a mad woman. Know her?'

Talfryn pointed upwards to the streaked sky.

'Dead?' said Roffrey.

'Gone,' Talfryn said. 'When the city started breaking

102

apart, she took one of the only ships and just spun off into space. She probably killed herself. She was like a zombie, and quite crazy. It was as if some outside pressure moved her. I heard she wanted to get to Roth. That was a crazy thing to want to do, in itself! She took one of the best ships, damn her. A nice one—Mark Seven Hauser.'

'She was heading for Roth? Isn't that the really strange planet?'

'As I said, she was crazy to go there. If she *did* get there.'

'You think there'd be a chance of her still being alive if she made it?'

'Maybe. Asquiol and Renark obviously survived.'

'Thanks for the information.' Roffrey turned away.

'Hey!' The skeleton suddenly became animated. 'You're not leaving us here! Take us with you—take us back to the fleet, for God's sake!'

Roffrey said: 'I'm not going back to the fleet. I'm going to Roth.'

'Then take us with you—anywhere's better than here!' Willow's voice was shrill and urgent.

Roffrey paused, deliberating. Then he said: 'Okay.'

As they neared the ship, something small and scaly scuttled across their path. It was like nothing Roffrey had seen before and he felt he never wanted to see it again. Entropium, when it flourished, had contained the seeds of corruption— and now corruption was dominant, a physical manifestation of a mental disease. It was an unhealthy place, with intelligent species scrabbling and fighting like animals to survive. It was rotten with the sickness that came from a state of mind as much as anything.

He was glad to reach the ship.

As Willow and Talfryn climbed into the airlock, he glanced back at the ruins, his face was rather grim. He helped them aboard and closed the lock.

Now he turned his thoughts to Mary the Maze.

TWELVE

Roffrey debated his next move, sitting hunched at the controls while he checked the astrochart before him. It didn't tally with the Shifter as it now was, but it would do. He could recognise descriptions of planets even though they had changed their location.

Willow and Talfryn were cleaning up. They were both beginning to look better. The ship itself was hardly tidy. It was not even very clean and there was a smell of the workshop about it—of oil, burnt rubber, dirty plastic and old leather. Roffrey liked it that way.

He scowled then. He didn't like company. *I'm getting soft,* he told himself.

Now he was going to Roth he began to feel nervous at what he might find there.

Talfryn said: 'We're ready!'

He activated the ship's normal drive and lifted off. He was tempted to burn the city to rubble as he passed, but he didn't. He got into space with a feeling of relief, heading in a series of flickering hops used for short journeys towards Roth, now hanging the farthest away from the parent binary, as if deliberately set apart from the rest of the system.

Roth, more than any other planet in the Shifter, defied the very logic of the cosmos and existed contrary to all laws. Roth—nicknamed Ragged Ruth, he remembered—still contained the impossible *gaps*. There, two men had become supersane. But Mary, poor Mary who had helped them—she had found only madness there.

Had she gone back to try and lay the ghost that was her insanity? Or had her motives been induced by madness? Perhaps he would find out.

The planet was big now. The screens showed nothing but the monstrous globe with its speckled aura, its shifting light-mist, its black blotches and, worst of all, the *gaps*. The *gaps* which were not so much seen as unseen. Something should be there but human eyes couldn't see it.

Roffrey flung the ship down through Roth's erratically tugging gravisphere, swinging down towards the unwelcoming surface which throbbed below like a sea of molten lava, changing and shifting like the seas of hell.

There seemed to be no consistent gravity. His instruments kept registering different findings. He fought to keep the descent as smooth as possible, concentrating on the operation, while Willow and Talfryn gasped and muttered, horrified by the vision.

He frowned, wondering what was familiar about the disturbing world. Then he remembered that the one time he had seen Renark and Asquiol they had possessed a similar quality, impossible to pin down, but as if their bodies had existed on different levels only just invisible to the human eye.

Yet this place was ominous. The men's images had been beautiful.

Ominous!

The word seethed around in his brain. Then, for one brief second, he passed through a warmth, a pleasure, a delight so exquisite yet so short-lived that it was as if he had lived and died in a moment.

He couldn't understand it. He had no time to try as the ship rocked in response to the weirdly unbalanced tug of Roth's gravity. He navigated with desperate skill, gliding low over the flame-mist boiling on the surface, trying without success to peer into the *gaps*, all his instruments operating on full power but few giving him any sensible readings, and lasers scanning the unstable surface.

Had Mary tried, perhaps like Renark, to find the Originators? Had something driven her back to the world that had turned her mad?

Then he spotted a ship on his screens, a ship surrounded by achingly disturbing light-mist. It was the Mark Seven Hauser. Mary's ship. And his energraph told him that the drive was active. That meant it had only recently landed or else was about to take off. He had to land fast!

He made planet-fall in a hurry, cursing the sudden grip of gravity for which he only just succeeded in compensating as he brought his ship close to the other vessel. His gauntleted fingers stabbed at buttons and he got into immediate contact with the Hauser on a tight laser beam.

'Anyone aboard?'

There was no reply.

Both Willow and Talfryn were peering at the screen now, bending over his shoulder.

'This ship seems to have arrived only recently,' he said.

It meant nothing to them and he realised that it meant little to him, either. He was pinning his hopes on too thin a circumstance.

He operated the laser, scanning as best he could the surrounding territory. Strange images jumped upon the screen, fading as rapidly as they approached. Harsh, craggy, crazy Roth, with its sickness of rock and the horror of the misty, intangible, unnatural *gaps*.

That men could survive here was astounding. Yet evidently they could. Asquiol and Mary had been living evidence. But it was easy to see how they went mad, hard to understand how they kept sane. It was a gaping, raw, boiling, dreadful world, emanating, it seemed, stark malevolence and baleful anger in its constant and turbulent motion.

Mary could easily have disappeared into one of the *gaps* or perished in some nameless way. His lips tightened as he left the screen and opened the spacesuit locker.

'If I need help I'll call you in my suit-phone,' he said as he picked up his discarded helmet. 'If you need them—suits are here.' He went to the airlock's elevator. 'I'll keep my suit-phone receiver on. If you see anything—any trace of Mary—let me know. Have the scanners working full-time.'

'You're a fool to go out there!' Talfryn said heavily.

'You're a non-participant in this,' Roffrey said savagely as he clamped his face-plate. 'Don't interfere. If it's obvious that I'm dead, you've got the ship to do what you like with. I've got to see what's in the Hauser.'

Now he was in the outer lock. Now he was lowering his body from the ship into a pool of yellow liquid that suddenly changed to shiny rock as he stepped on to it. Something slid and itched beneath his feet.

His lips were dry, the skin of his face seemed cracked and brittle. His eyes kept focusing and unfocusing. But the most disturbing thing of all was the silence. All his instincts told him that the ghastly changes taking place on the surface should make *noise*. But they didn't. This heightened the dreamlike quality of his motion over the shifting surface.

In a moment, his own ship could no longer be seen and he reached the Hauser, noting that the lock was wide open. Both locks were open when he got inside. Gas of some kind swirled through the ship. He went into the cabin and found traces of the pilot having been there recently. There were some figures scribbled on a pad beside the chart-viewer. The equations were incomprehensible—but they were in Mary's writing!

A quick search through the ship told him nothing more. Hastily he pulled himself through the cabin door and down the airlock shaft until he was again on the surface. He peered with difficulty through the shifting flame-mist. It was thoroughly unnerving. But he forced himself through it, blindly searching for a mad woman who could have gone anywhere.

Then two figures emerged out of the mist and, just as suddenly, merged back into it.

He was sure he recognised one of them. He called after them. They didn't reply. He began to follow but lost sight of them.

Then a piercing shout blasted into his suit-phone.

'Asquiol! Oh, Asquiol!'

He whirled around. It was the voice of Willow Kovacs. Was Asquiol looking for him? Had the fleet been defeated? If so, why had the two men ignored his shout?

'Asquiol! Come back! It's me, Willow!'

But Roffrey wanted to find Mary the Maze; he wasn't interested in Asquiol. He began to run, plunging through hallucinations, through shapes that formed silently around him as if to engulf him, through turquoise tunnels, up mauve mountains. In places, gravity was low and he bounded along; in others it became almost impossible to drag his bulk.

Now he entered another low gravity patch and bounded with bone-jarring suddenness into a heavy one. Painfully he lifted his booted feet, barely able to support his heavy body.

Then a voice—perhaps through his suit-phone, perhaps not. He recognised the voice. His heart leapt.

'It's warm, warm, warm . . . Where now? Here . . . but . . . Let me go back . . . Let me . . .'

It was Mary's voice.

For a moment he didn't respond to the shock. His mouth was dry, his features petrified. His body was frozen as he strained to hear the voice again.

'Mary—where are you?'

It was as if he were experiencing an awful dream where menace threatened but he was unable to escape, where every

107

step seemed to take every ounce of energy and every scrap of time he possessed.

Again he croaked: 'Mary!'

But it was not for some minutes that heard the reply:

'Keep moving! Don't stop. Don't stop!'

He didn't know whether the words were addressed to him or not, but he thought it best to obey then.

He began to sway and fall down, but he kept moving. Then it was as if the whole planet were above him and he was like Atlas, slowly crumpling beneath its weight.

He screamed.

Then Willow's voice blasted through: '*Asquiol! Asquiol!*'

What was happening? It was all too confusing. He couldn't grasp . . . He felt faint. He looked *up* and saw several small figures scurrying across the planet he held with his hands. Then he was growing, growing, growing . . .

Again he screamed. A hollow, echoing roar in his ears.

His heart beat a frantic rhythm against his rib-cage until his ears became filled with the noise. He panted and struggled, crawling up over the curved surface of the planet, hanging on to it as if by his fingernails.

He was a great giant, larger than the tiny planet—but at the same time he was a flea, crawling through syrup and cotton-wool.

He laughed then in his madness.

He laughed and stopped abruptly, grasping for the threads of sanity and pulling them together. He was standing in a light gravity patch and things suddenly looked as normal as they could on Roth.

He glanced through a patch in the mist and saw Mary standing there. He ran towards her.

'Mary!'

'*Asquiol!*'

The woman was Willow Kovacs in a suit—Mary's old suit. He made as if to strike her down, but the look of disappointment on her face stopped him. He pushed past her, changed his mind, came back.

'Willow—Mary's here, I know . . .' Suddenly he realised the possible truth. 'My God, of course. Time's so twisted and warped we could be seeing anything that's happened at any time in the past—or the future!'

Another figure came stumbling out of the light-mist. It was Talfryn.

'I couldn't contact you from the ship. There's a woman there. She . . .'

'It's an illusion, man. Get back to the ship!'

'You come with me. It's no illusion. She entered the ship herself!'

'Lead the way back,' Roffrey said. Willow remained where she was, refusing to budge. At length they had to lift her, squirming, and carry her back. It was only three yards away.

The woman wore a space suit. She was lying on the floor of the cabin. Roffrey bent over her, lifting the face-plate.

'Mary,' he said, softly. 'Mary—thank God!'

The eyes opened, the big soft eyes that had once held intelligence. For a short time intelligence was there—a look of incredible awareness. Then it faded and she formed her lips to say something, but they twisted downwards into an idiot grin and she subsided into a blank-eyed daze.

He got up wearily, his body bowed. He made a gesture with his left hand. 'Willow, help her out of the suit. We'll get her into a bunk.'

Willow looked at him with hatred: 'Asquiol's out there . . . You stopped me.'

Talfryn said: 'Even if he was he wouldn't want you. You keep pining for him, wishing you'd followed him earlier. Now it's too late. It's no good, Willow, you've lost him for ever!'

'Once he sees me he'll take me back. He loved me!'

Roffrey said impatiently to Talfryn: 'You'd better help me, then.'

Talfryn nodded. They began getting her out of the suit.

'Willow,' said Roffrey as they worked, 'Asquiol wasn't there—not now. You saw something that probably happened years ago. The other man was Renark—and Renark's dead? You understand?'

'I saw him. He heard me call him!'

'Maybe. I don't know. Don't worry Willow. We're going back to the fleet if we can—if it still exists. You'll see him then.'

Talfryn wrenched off a piece of space-armour from Mary's body with a savage movement. His teeth were clenched but he said nothing.

'You're going back to the fleet? But you said . . .' Willow was disconcerted. Roffrey noted a peculiar look, a mixture of eagerness and introspection.

'Mary needs treatment. The only place she'll get it is back there. So that's where I'm going. That should suit you.'

'It does,' she said. 'Yes, it does.'

He went over to the ports and closed their shutters so they couldn't see Roth's surface. It felt a little safer.

Talfryn said suddenly: 'I get it, Willow. You've made it plain. I won't be bothering you from now on.'

'You'd better not.' She turned on Roffrey: 'And that goes for you, too, for any man. I'm Asquiol's woman, as you'll see when we get back to the fleet!'

'Don't worry,' he grinned. 'You're not my type.'

She pushed back her lank hair, piqued. 'Thanks,' she said.

Roffrey smiled at Mary, who sat drooling and crooning in her bunk. He winked at her. 'You're my type, Mary,' he said genially.

'That's cruel,' Willow said sharply.

'That's my wife.' Roffrey smiled, and then Willow saw at least a trace of what the smiling eyes and grin hid.

She turned away.

'Let's get going,' said Roffrey briskly. Now that he had made up his mind, he wanted to waste no time returning to the fleet.

He couldn't guess how long Mary had been on Roth. Maybe only a few minutes of real time. Maybe a hundred years of Roth's time. He did not allow himself to dwell on this, just as he refused to consider the extent of her mental derangement. The phychiatrists in the fleet might soon be supplying him with all the information they possibly could. He was prepared to wait and see.

He went over to her. She shrank away from him, muttering and crooning, her big eyes wider than ever. Very gently he made her lie down in the bunk and strapped her into it with safety harness. It pained him that she didn't recognise him, but he was still smiling and humming a little tune to himself as he climbed into the pilot's seat, heaved back a lever, adjusted a couple of dials, flipped a series of switches and soon the drone of the drive was drowning his own humming.

Then, in a flicker, they were off into deep space and heading away from the Sundered Worlds into the depths of matterless void. It was such an easy lift-off, Roffrey felt, that it was almost as if a friendly hand had given them a push from behind . . .

It was with a sense of inevitability that he began the descent through the dimension layers, heading back to the space-time in which he'd left the fleet of mankind.

Meanwhile, men's brains were jarred and jumbled as they strove to master the Game. Minds broke. Nerves snapped. But, while scarcely understanding what it was about, Lord Mordan forced his team to continue, convinced that humanity's chance of survival depended on winning . . .

Whistling sounds were the first impressions Roffrey received as he phased the ship out of the Shifter's space-time and into the next level.

Space around them suddenly became bright with stars, the not-quite-familiar whirl of a spiral galaxy searing outwards in a wild sprawl of suns. But the whistle was replaced by a dreadful moaning which pervaded the ship and made speech impossible.

Roffrey was intent on the new instruments. The little experience he had of the continuum-travelling device had shown him that the ship could easily slip back through the space-time layers and become totally lost.

The instrument's hadn't been designed for wide travelling of this kind and Roffrey knew it, but each separate universe in the multiverse had its particular co-ordinates, and the instruments, crude as they were, could differentiate between them. Over the main laser screen Roffrey had a chart which would enable him to recognise the universe into which the human race had fled. But the journey could be dangerous, perhaps impossible.

And then the noise increased to become painful, no longer a monotone but a pulsating, nerve-racking whine. Roffrey phased into the next layer.

The galaxy ahead was a seething inferno of unformed matter, hazy, bright, full of archetypal colour—reds, whites, blacks, yellows—pouring about in slow disorder. This was a universe in a state of either birth or dissolution.

There was near-silence as Roffrey phased out of this continuum and into the next. His whistling, which he had been doing all the while, was light and cheerful. Then he heard Mary's groans and he stopped.

Now they were in the centre of a galaxy.

Massed stars lay in all directions. He stared at them in

wonder, noticing how, with every phase, the matter, filling the space around them seemed to change its position as well as its nature.

Then the stars were gone and he was passing through a turbulent mass of dark gas which seemed to form into horrible half-recognisable shapes which sickened him so that he could no longer look but had to concentrate on his instruments.

What he read there depressed and shocked him!

He was off course.

He chewed at his moustache, debating what to do. He didn't mention it to the others. The co-ordinates corresponded to those on the chart above the screen.

As far as the ship's instruments were concerned, they were in the space-time occupied by Asquiol and the fleet!

Yet it was totally different from what he remembered. Gas swirled in it and he could not see the stars of the galaxy.

Had the fleet been completely wiped out?

There was no other explanation.

Then he cursed as the black gas suddenly became alive, a roaring and monstrous beast, many-tendrilled, dark blue, flame-eyed, malevolent. Willow and Talfryn gasped behind him as they saw it loom on the screen. Mary began shrieking, the sounds filled the cabin. The ship was heading straight towards the monster. But how could something like this exist in the near-vacuum of space?

Roffrey didn't have time for theories. He broke the energy seals of his anti-neutron cannon as an acrid smell filled the cabin and the beast rapidly changed from deep blue to startling yellow.

The guns swung on the beast and Roffrey stabbed the firing buttons, then backed the ship away savagely.

The ship shuddered as the guns sent a deadly stream of anti-neutrons towards the monster. Meanwhile, the beast seemed, impossibly, to be absorbing the beams and new heads had grown on its shoulders—disgusting, half-human faces gibbering and yelling, and they could *hear* the cries! Roffrey felt and tasted bile in his throat.

Talfryn was now bending over him, staring at the screen.

'What is it?' he shouted above Mary's screams.

'How the hell should I know?' Roffrey said viciously. He righted the ship's backward velocity, stabbed the cannon buttons again. He heaved his big body round in the control seat and said: 'Make yourself useful, Talfryn. See if the co-ordinates on that chart tally absolutely with those on this screen.'

The monster lurched through the dark mist towards the little launch, its heads drooling and grinning. There wasn't time to wonder what it was, how it existed.

Roffrey aimed at its main head. He began to depress the firing button.

Then it had gone.

There were a few wisps of gas in the dark, sharp space of the galaxy Roffrey immediately recognised.

They were in the right galaxy!

But now a new danger threatened. Replacing the monster was a squadron of fast, spherical vessels—those he had glimpsed just before leaving the fleet. Were they the victors, cleaning up the last of the race. They were passing on the zenith-south flank of Roffrey's battered launch. He trailed the ship round on a tight swing so that he was now directly facing the oncoming alien ships.

The launch was responding well, but the cabin shook and rattled as he stood his vessel on a column of boiling black fire and glided away from the round ships, having shot a tremendous burst towards them. Something was disturbing him. He found it hard to concentrate properly. Talfryn was obviously having the same trouble. A quick look behind him showed Mary's gaping mouth as she screamed and screamed.

Talfryn clung instinctively to the hand-grip and shouted: 'The co-ordinates tally perfectly.'

'That's news?' Roffrey said lightly.

Willow had joined Mary and was attempting to comfort her. Mary was rigid, staring ahead of her with fixed, glazed eyes. It was as if she could see something that was invisible to the others. Her screams rang on, a horrible ululation in the confined cabin.

Willow peered through the bad light at the two men half-silhouetted up ahead, the one in the control seat, the other standing over him, their dark clothes picked out against the spluttering brightness of the screens and instruments, their faces in shadow, their hands white on the controls.

The lighting was very dim as all power-sources were drained to provide the ship with maximum power.

She looked out of the nearest port. Space was blank—suddenly colourless. She looked back at the men and her vision was engulfed by a horrible disharmony of colour and noise, sense impressions of all kinds—obscene, primeval, terrible—throwing her mind into disorder so that she found it almost impossible to differentiate between her five senses.

Then, when she had completely lost her ability to tell whether she was smelling or hearing a colour, her head was filled with a single impression that combined as one thing to her sense: Smell, sight, touch, sound and taste were all there, but the combination produced a unified sense that all were blood red.

She thought she was dead.

Roffrey shouted and the sound hung alone for a moment before he saw it merge into the blood red disharmony. He felt madness approach and then recede—approach and recede, like a horrible tide, for with each sweep it came a little closer. His body vibrated with the tension, sending out clouds of blood red trailers through the cabin which he saw—no, he heard it, as the note of a muted trumpet. It horrified him, for now something else was creeping through, something coming up from his oldest memories, something of which he hadn't even been aware.

He was immersed in self-loathing, self-pity, suddenly knowing what a debased thing he was . . .

But there was something—he didn't know what—aiding him in spite of his confusion, aiding him to cling to his personal being, to sweat out the tumble of disordered impressions and terrible thoughts, and to hit back.

He hit back!

Mary was still quivering in Willow's arms—taut, tense, no longer screaming.

The waves began to peter out.

Willow struck, too. Struck back at whatever it was that was doing this to them.

The waves faded and, slowly, their senses were restored to normal.

Suddenly Mary's body relaxed. She had passed out. Talfryn was slumped on the floor and Roffrey was hunched in the control seat, growling.

He peered through the rapidly fading pulsations and saw with satisfaction that the anti-neutrons had done their job, though he hadn't been able to direct them properly, nor had he been fully conscious of directing them.

Some of the ships were making off, others were warped

lumps of metal spinning aimlessly in the void. He began whistling to himself as he adjusted the controls. The whistling died as he said:

'You all right back there?'

Willow said: 'What do you think, superman? Mary and Paul have passed out. Mary took it worse than any of us—she seemed to bear the brunt of it. What was it, do you think?'

'I don't know. Maybe we'll get our answers soon.'

'Why?'

'I've sighted our fleet!'

'Thank God,' said Willow, and she began to tremble. She dared not anticipate her reunion with Asquiol.

Roffrey headed for the fleet—going back as fast as he'd left.

THIRTEEN

The fleet had been badly depleted since he left it. It was still big—a sprawling collection of ships, stretching mile upon mile in all directions and resembling nothing so much as a vast scrap-yard, guarded by the cruising Geepee battle-wagons like whales guarding a motley school of fish.

In the centre of the fleet, a little distance from Asquiol's battered cruiser (easily recognised by its slightly out-of-focus outline) was a huge factory ship with the letters 'G' emblazoned on its side. This puzzled Roffrey.

Then the Geepee patrol contacted him.

To his astonishment, he had the pleasure of being received almost cordially. They began to guide him into a position fairly close to the factory ship with the 'G' on its side.

While Roffrey was getting his ship into line, a man in the loose, unmilitary garb which was identical save for rank insignia with all other Geepee uniforms, appeared on the laser screen, his stern, bloodhound face puzzled. The large band on his left sleeve also bore a letter 'G'.

'Hello, Lord Mordan,' Roffrey said with cheerful defiance.

Willow wondered at the vitality and control which Roffrey must possess in order to seem suddenly so relaxed and untroubled.

Lord Mordan smiled ironically. 'Good morning. So you decided to return and help us after all. Where have you been?'

'I've been on a mercy trip rescuing survivors from the Shifter,' Roffrey said virtuously.

'I don't believe you,' Mordan said candidly. 'But I don't care—you've just done something nobody thought was possible. As soon as we assemble our data I'll be getting in touch with you again. We need all the help we can get in this business—even yours. We're up against it, Roffrey. We're damn near finished.' He broke off as if to pull himself together. 'Now, if you *are* carrying extra passengers, you'd better register them with the appropriate authorities.' He switched out.

'What did all that mean?' said Talfryn.

'I don't know,' Roffrey said, 'but we may find out soon. Mordan obviously knows something. The fleet's evidently suffered from attacks such as we experienced. Yet there seems to be more order now. The battle, or whatever it is, seems to have taken a different course.'

Willow Kovacs cradled Mary Roffrey's head in her arm and gently wiped a trickle of saliva from the mad woman's mouth. Her heart was beating swiftly and her stomach seemed contracted, her arms and legs weak. She was very frightened now at the prospect of reunion with Asquiol. Surely he had remained faithful to her.

Roffrey locked the ship's controls and came aft, staring down at the two women with a light smile on his sensuous, bearded mouth. He began stripping off his suit and the overalls beneath, revealing a plain quilted jacket of maroon plastileather and grubby white trousers tucked into soft leather knee-boots.

'How's Mary?'

'I don't know,' Willow said. 'She's obviously not sane . . . Yet there's a different quality about her insanity. Something I can't pin down.'

'A doctor maybe will help,' Roffrey said. He patted Willow's shoulder. 'Contact the admin ship will you, Talfryn? Send out a general call till you can get it.'

'Okay,' Talfryn said.

Worst of all, Roffrey thought as he stared down at his wife, had been the all-pervading red—blood red. It had been

116

unmistakable as blood red. Why had it affected him so badly. What had it done to Mary?

He scratched the back of his neck. He hadn't slept since he left the fleet. He was full of stimulants, but he felt the need for some natural sleep. Maybe later.

When Talfryn had contacted the Registration Ship, which had as its job the classification of all members of the fleet so that it would be easier to administer the survivors if they at last made planet-fall, they were told that an official would be sent over in a short while.

Roffrey said: 'We need a psychiatrist of some sort, quickly. Can you help?'

'Try a hospital ship—though it's unlikely you'll be lucky.'

He tried a hospital ship. The doctor in charge wasn't helpful.

'No, I'm afraid you won't get a psychiatrist for your wife. If you need medical treatment we'll put her on our list. We're overworked. It's impossible to deal with all the casualties . . .'

'But you've got to help her!' Roffrey bellowed.

The doctor didn't argue. He just switched out.

Roffrey, bewildered by this, swung round in his chair. Willow and Talfryn were discussing the earlier conflict with the alien ships.

'They must be hard pushed,' Roffrey cursed. 'But I'm going to get help for Mary even if it means going right to the top.'

'But what about those hallucinations we had back there?' Talfryn said. 'What caused them?'

'It's my guess we were experiencing the force of one of their weapons,' Roffrey replied. 'Maybe what happened to us on Roth made us more susceptible to hallucination.'

'A weapon—yes, it could be.'

The communicator buzzed. Talfryn went to it.

'Registration,' said a jaunty voice. 'Mind if I come aboard?'

He was a pale and perky midget with genial eyes and a very neat appearance. His gig clamped against Roffrey's airlock and he came bustling through with a case of papers under his arm.

'You would be Captain Adam Roffrey,' he lisped, staring up at the black-bearded giant.

Roffrey stared down at him, half in wonder.

'I would be.'

'Good. And you embarked with the rest of the human race roughly two weeks ago—relative time, that is. I don't know how long it was in *your* time, since it is not always possible to leave and return from one dimension to another and keep the time flow the same—kindly remember that.'

'I'll try,' said Roffrey, wondering if there was a question there.

'And these three are . . .?'

'Miss Willow Kovacs, formerly of Migaa . . .'

The midget scribbled in his notebook, looking prim at the mention of the planet Migaa. It had possessed something of a reputation in the home galaxy.

Willow gave the rest of her data. Talfryn gave his.

'And the other lady?' The little official asked.

'My wife—Doctor Mary Roffrey, born on Earth, née Ishenko; anthropologist; disappeared from Golund on the Rim in 457 Galactic General Time, reappeared from Shifter System a short while ago. The Geepees will have all her details prior to her disappearance. I gave them to the police when she disappeared. As usual, they did nothing.'

The midget frowned, then darted a look at Mary.

'State of health?'

'Insane,' said Roffrey, quietly.

'Curable or otherwise?'

'Curable!' said Roffrey, and the word was cold, savage.

The tiny official completed his notes, thanked them all and was about to leave when Roffrey said:

'Just a minute. Could you fill me in on what's happened to the fleet since I left?'

'As long as we keep it brief, I'd be pleased to. Remember, I'm a busy little man!' He giggled.

'Just before we got here we had a tussle with some alien ships, experienced hallucinations, and so on. Do you know what that was?'

'No wonder the lady is insane! For untrained people to withstand the pressure, it's amazing! Wait till I tell my colleagues! You're heroes! You survived a wild round!'

'Bully for us. What happened?'

'Well, I'm only a petty official—they don't come much pettier than me—but from what I've *gathered,* you had a "wild round." That is,' he explained quickly, 'anyone straying beyond the confines of the fleet is attacked by the aliens and has to play a wild round, as we call it—one that isn't

118

scheduled to be played by the Gamblers. We're not really supposed to do that.'

'But what *is* this Game?'

'I'm not sure, really. Ordinary people don't play the Game —only the Gamblers in the Game Ship. That's the one with the big "G" on it. It isn't the sort of game I'd like to play. We call it the Blood Red Game because of the habit they have of confusing our sense so that everything seems to be the colour of blood. Psychologists and the like play it and they are called Gamblers . . .'

'How often is it played?'

'All the time, really. No wonder I'm a bundle of nerves. We all are. Citizen's rights have been waived, food supplies reduced . . . We're having a pause just at the moment, but it won't last long. Probably they're recovering from your little victory.'

'Who'd know details about this Game?'

'Asquiol, of course, but it's almost impossible to see him. The nearest people ever get is to his airlock, and then only rarely. You might try Lord Mordan, though he's not too approachable, either. Mr. High and Mighty—he's worse than Asquiol in some ways.'

'Mordan seems interested enough to tell us already,' Roffrey nodded. 'But I've got to speak to Asquiol on another matter, so I might as well try to combine them. Thanks.'

'A pleasure,' the midget enthused.

When he had gone, Roffrey went to the communicator and tried to contact Asquiol's ship. He had to get by nearly a dozen officials before he made contact.

'Adam Roffrey here, just in from the Shifter. Can I come to your ship?'

He received a curt acceptance. There had been no picture.

'Will you take me with you?' Willow asked. 'He'll be surprised. I've been waiting a long, long time for this. He predicted we might meet again, and he was right.'

'Of course,' Roffrey agreed. He looked at Talfryn. 'He was a friend of yours, too. Want to come?'

Talfryn shook his head. 'I'll stay here and try to find out a bit more about what's going on here.' He took a long, almost theatrical look at Willow and then turned away. 'See you.'

Roffrey said: 'Just as you like.' He went to the medical

chest and took out a hypodermic and a bottle of sedative, filled the hypo and pumped the stuff into Mary's arm.

Then he and Willow left his launch and, by means of personal power units, made their way to Asquiol's ship.

The airlock was open, ready for them, and it closed behind them as the entered. The inner lock, however, did not open.

Instead, they saw the light of an internal viewer blink on as they waited and they heard a brooding voice—a polite, faraway voice that seemed to carry peculiar echoes which their ears could not quite catch.

'Asquiol speaking. How may I help you?'

Willow, masked in her space-suit, remained silent.

'I'm Adam Roffrey, just in from the Shifter system with three passengers.'

'Yes?' Asquiol's acknowledgement bore no trace of interest.

'One of them is my wife—you know her as Mary the Maze. She helped Renark in the Shifter.' Roffrey paused. 'She sent you to Roth.'

'I am grateful to her, though we didn't meet.'

'I've tried to contact a psychiatrist in the fleet. I haven't succeeded.' Roffrey kept his voice level. 'I don't know where they all are, but my wife's condition is desperate. Can you help?'

'They are all playing the Game. I am sorry. Grateful as I am to your wife the first priority is to the race. We cannot release a psychiatrist.'

Roffrey was shocked. He had expected some response at least. 'Not even to give me advice how to help her?'

'No. You must do what you can for her yourself. Perhaps a medical man will be able to give you certain kinds of help.'

Roffrey turned disgustedly back towards the outer lock. He stopped as Asquiol's voice came again: 'I suggest you contact Lord Mordan as soon as you can.'

The voice cut off.

'Willow spoke. She felt as if she had died and the word was the last she would ever utter.

'*Asquiol!*'

At length, they returned to Roffrey's ship.

Mary was sleeping peacefully under the sedative but Talfryn had disappeared. They did not bother to wonder where he had gone. They sat by Mary's bunk, both of them depressed, their thoughts turned inward.

'He's changed,' Willow said flatly.

Roffrey grunted.

'He doesn't sound human any longer,' she said. 'There's no way of appealing to him. He doesn't seem to care about the approval of the rest of us. His loyalty to these mysterious creatures he contacted seems greater than his loyalty to his friends—or the rest of mankind, for that matter.'

Roffrey stared down at Mary..

'He doesn't care about anything except this "mission" he has. Everything is being sacrificed and subordinated to that one aim. I don't even know how valid it is. If I did I might be able to argue—or even agree with him!'

'Perhaps Paul could talk to him. I got scared. I meant to tell him who I was. I might be able to later.'

'Save it. I'll see what Mordan wants with me first.'

Roffrey moved over to his control panel and operated the screen.

'Lord Mordan?'

'Mordan here.' The Gee-lord's face appeared on the screen. He seemed disconcerted when he saw Roffrey.

'I was just going to contact you. You and Talfryn have been enlisted as Gamblers—subject to preliminary tests.'

'What the hell, Mordan? I'm not interested. Tell Talfryn about it. I've got a sick wife to think about.'

'Talfryn's already here.' Mordan's face was serious. 'This is important—though it may not look like it to you. There's a war to the death on and we're up against it. I'm directly responsible to Asquiol for enlisting any men I think will help us win. You've given us a great deal of trouble already. I'm empowered to kill anyone liable to disrupt our security. Come over to the Game Ship—and come fast! If you refuse we'll bring you over forcibly. Clear?'

Roffrey switched out without answering.

Defiantly, he waited by Mary's bed. She was beginning to show signs of improving, physically, but how her mind would be when she came out of the drugged sleep he didn't know.

Later, two Geepees demanded entry. Their launch was clamped fast against his. They threatened to hole his ship and enter that way if they had to. He opened the airlocks and let them in.

'What can one extra hand do?' he said.

One of them replied: 'Any man who can hold off an

enemy attack virtually single-handed is needed in the Game Ship. That's all we know.'

'But I didn't . . .' Roffrey stopped himself. He was losing his grip.

The Geepee said with false impatience: 'You may not have realised it, Captain Roffrey, but you did something a while ago that was impossible. You held out under the combined attack, mental and physical, of ten enemy ships. Most people couldn't have taken an attack from even one!'

The other Geepee drawled: 'That means something. Look at it this way. We're damn near beaten now. We took a hell of a lambasting during the initial alien attacks. We're the last survivors of the human race and we've got to stay together, work for the common good. That's the only way you'll look after your wife in the long run. Don't you see that?'

Roffrey was still not convinced. He was a stubborn man. There was an atavistic impulse in him which had always kept him away from the herd, and outside the law, relying entirely on his own initiative and wits. But he was also an intelligent man so he nodded slightly and said:

'Very well—I'll speak to Lord Mordan, anyway.' Then he turned to Willow. 'Willow, if Mary shows any sign of getting worse, let me know.'

'Of course, Adam.'

'You'll stay with her—make sure she's all right?'

She looked into his face. 'Naturally. But when she's under a sedative there's something else I've got to do.'

'Yes. I understand.'

He shrugged at the Geepees, who turned and led him through the airlock.

FOURTEEN

The Game Ship was bigger than a large battle-wagon, even more functional-looking, a little barer of comforts. Yet it did not seem prepared for battle. There was an atmosphere of hushed silence aboard and their boots clanged loudly along the corridor which led to Lord Mordan's cabin.

A sign on the door read: *Deputy Game Master, Lord*

Mordan. Strictly Private. The letters were heavy black on the white door.

The Geepee accompanying Roffrey knocked on the door.

'Enter!'

They went through into a cabin cluttered with instruments.

There were some Roffrey recognised—an encephalograph, an optigraph-projector—machines for measuring the power of the brain, equipment for testing visualising capacity, for measuring I.Q. potential, and so on.

Talfryn was sitting in a comfortable chair on the other side of Mordan's desk. Both men had their hands clenched before them—Talfryn's in his lap, Mordan's stretched out across the empty desk.

'Sit down, Roffrey,' said Lord Mordan. He made no reference to Roffrey's defiance of orders. He seemed perfectly controlled. Perhaps over-controlled, thought Reffrey. For a moment he sympathised—wasn't that his own condition?'

He sat down as the Geepee guard left.

'Okay,' he said curtly. 'Get on with it.'

'I've been explaining to Talfryn how important you both are to this project,' Mordan said crisply. 'Are you prepared to go along with us on the first stage of our tests?'

'Yes.' He was almost responding to the decisive mood.

'Good. We've got to find out exactly what qualities you possessed which made defeat of that alien fleet possible. There is a chance, of course, that you were lucky, or that being unprepared for the sense-impression attack on you and having no understanding of its origin, you were psychologically better prepared to meet the attack. We'll know the answers later. Let me recap on recent events first.'

Mordan spoke rapidly :

'As you know, we entered this universe several weeks ago and encountered its inhabitants shortly after entry. These people are non-human, as might be expected, and regard us as invaders. That's fair enough, since we should think the same in their position. But they made no attempt to assess our potential strength, to parley or order us away. They attacked. We have no idea even what they look like, these aliens. You saw how quickly they had mobilised an attack on our fleet, well before we had a chance to talk and tell them why we are here.'

'What happened after the first battle—the one I saw?'

'There were several others. We lost a lot of ships of all

kinds. Finally, Asquiol contacted them by his own methods, and intimated that we were quite prepared to settle on planets unsuitable for them and live in friendly co-operation with them. But they wouldn't accept this. However, they came up with an alternative to open·warfare.' He sighed and waved his hand to indicate the massed equipment.

'We did not reckon with the predominant society existing here. It is based on a Code of Behaviour which we find, in parts, very difficult to grasp.

'In our terms it means that the status of a particular individual or group is decided by its ability to play a warlike game which has been played in this galaxy for centuries. We call it the Blood Red Game, since one of their prime "weapons" is the ability to addle our sense-impressions so that we get a total sensory experience of the colour red. You already know this, I believe.'

Roffrey agreed. 'But what, apart from confusing us, is it meant to do? And how does it work?'

'We believe that the aliens have come to rely, when disputes break out among themselves, on more subtle weapons than energy-cannon or anything similar. If we wished, we might continue to use our familiar weapons to fight them, as we did at first. But we should have only a slight chance of winning. Their weapons make you better than dead, in their view. They turn you insane. If you were dead you'd be out of the way. But since you're alive but useless as a fighter, you drain our resources and slow us down in many ways. But that's only part of it. There are rigid, complicated rules which we are having to learn as we go along.'

'What are the stakes?' Roffrey asked.

'If we win so many rounds of the Game without relying on our ordinary armaments, the aliens will concede us the right to rule, as absolute monarchs, their galaxy! Big stakes, Captain Roffrey. We lose our lives, they lose their power.'

'They must be confident of winning.'

'Not according to Asquiol. The fact that they *are* winning at the moment is obvious, but their love of playing this Game is so ingrained that they welcome any new variety. You see, both sides have got to do more than simply play the Game, they have the added difficulty of not understanding the opponent's capabilities, susceptibilities, psychology and so forth. In that, we're even. In other things, such as experience of playing the Game, they have the advantage.'

'Where do we come into this?'

'We're hoping that you are the aces we need in order to win. Your ship was the only human ship which has ever succeeded in beating the fantastic odds. Somehow, you have something we need to beat the aliens!'

'And you don't know what it is?'

'Right.'

'Do we possess it jointly—or does only one of us possess this protective "shield-attack" quality, whatever it is?'

'We're going to find that out, Captain Roffrey. That's why we're testing you both. Although you were actually at the controls of your ship, Talfryn, I understand, was beside you.'

Talfryn spoke slowly: 'What we have to seek, I gather, is a *moral* advantage over the aliens. It is not a question of numbers but prestige. If we win, we gain sufficient status for them to accept our dominance. If we lose . . . what?'

'If we lose, we'll be beyond caring. Our supplies are so short we can't risk phasing into a new universe at this late stage.' Lord Mordan turned his attention back to Roffrey. 'Do you see that, captain? Your wife is only one of a few victims of insanity in the fleet at the moment. But if we don't win the Game, we'll all be mad—or dead.'

Roffrey understood the logic. But he was still suspicious of it.

'Let's get these tests over with,' he said. 'Then maybe we'll know where we're going. I'll make up my mind afterwards.'

Mordan tightened his lips, nodding a trifle. 'As you like,' he said. He spoke towards his desk. 'Ask the testing team to come here.'

Three men entered Mordan's cluttered cabin.

Mordan stood up to introduce them.

'This is Professor Selinsky,' he said. The tallest of the group detached himself and walked over to Roffrey and Talfryn. He stretched out his fat hand and smiled warmly.

'Glad you're here,' he said. 'It looks as if you and your friend may be able to help us out of our present difficulties.'

He shook hands with them and said: 'These are my assistants. Doctor Zung'—a small, gloomy man of Mongolian appearance—'and Doctor Mann'—a young, blond-headed man who looked like an adventure-fiction hero.

'I've heard of you, professor,' said Talfryn. 'You used to hold the Chair of Physiology at Earth.'

'That's right,' Selinsky nodded. Then he said. 'We'll give you an ordinary test with the electro-encephalograph first. Then we'll put you to sleep and see if we can get at the subconscious. You're prepared to accept all our tests, I presume.' He looked at Mordan who made no reply.

Roffrey said: 'Yes. As long as it doesn't involve brainwashing.'

Selinsky said sternly: 'This is the fifth century, you know —not the fifth century pre-war.'

'I thought Asquiol and Lord Mordan's motto had become *Needs Must When The Devil Drives,*' Roffrey said as he sat in the seat which Doctor Zung had prepared for him.

But the reference made no impression on Mordan who had probably never heard it. Roffrey was given to obscure quotations—it was all part of his atavistic outlook. Mary had once accused him of being deliberately obscurist in his references, of reading old books merely in order to pick up unfamiliar quotations to fling at people he despised or disliked. He had agreed. Part of her attraction, he had added, was that she, at least, knew what he was talking about.

A small, glass-alloy helmet was now being fitted over his scalp. He hated such devices. He hated it all. As soon as this is over, he promised himself, I'll show them what independence really means.

Such thoughts and emotions gave the scientists some interesting, if hardly usable, findings.

Professor Selinsky appeared calm as he checked over the material so far gained from the sleeping men.

'All this will require careful analysis, of course,' he said. Then he shrugged his shoulders.

'What have you found out?' Mordan said.

'Frankly, I can't find any clue at first sight as to what they've got that men we're using haven't already got. They're both intelligent—Roffrey quite superlatively so, but there's only a grain of something out of the ordinary. Naturally, this quality would be subtle—we expected that—but Roffrey isn't the only psychopath in the human race and he isn't the only one with a high I.Q.' He sighed.

'But their memories for sensory-experiences are very good,' Doctor Mann said eagerly. 'In any event they will help swell the Gambling strength.'

'A poor second,' said Zung disgustedly as he uncoupled electrodes and neatly placed his personal equipment in its cases. 'I'll agree that we need all the Gamblers we can recruit—but these men were going to give us the answer to the problem of defeating the aliens. That's what we hoped, didn't we, professor?'

Selinsky said: 'This project is wearing us all down, Zung. There's not a scrap of reason for your defeatest tone—nor yours, Mann. We have a lot of work to do before we can analyse our findings. Meanwhile'—he turned to Mordan who had been sitting in his chair with a look of studied indifference on his seamed, bloodhound's face—'I suggest we put these men on our regular strength. No need to waste them while we study their results. Let them be trained.'

'You're sure they'll work all right with the rest?' Mordan said, getting up.

'Why shouldn't they?' Selinsky pointed his thumb towards the door. 'You know what the atmosphere in there's like, with O'Hara and everything . . . None of them are what you would call "normal." Our Gamblers are all neurotics these days, by definition. Normal people couldn't stand the strain—normal people couldn't hit back. We count on unusual physiological and psychological patterns to play the Game.'

'I trust Talfryn,' Mordan said, 'he's much more susceptible to persuasion. But Roffrey's a born troublemaker. I know—I've dealt with him more than once.'

'Give him something important to handle, in that case.' Selinsky swung the arm of the optigraph away from Roffrey's chair. The man stirred but didn't wake. 'He's the kind who needs to be kept active—who needs to feel that every action he makes is personally inspired.'

'There never was such a thing,' said Mordan, walking over and staring down at his old enemy.

'Then don't tell him.' Selinsky smiled faintly. 'It's egocentricity of that order which has pushed humanity up the scale. Renark and Asquiol were the same—they may sometimes have the wrong information, but they get better results than we do.'

'Of a kind,' Mordan agreed reluctantly.

'It's the kind we need right now,' Selinsky told him as he and his assistants bustled out of the cabin. 'We'll send a couple of attendants to take care of them.'

'You'll need the whole damn police force to take care of Roffrey once he starts getting stubborn,' Mordan said fatalistically. He liked Roffrey, but he knew Roffrey didn't like him. He'd come to the somewhat comforting conclusion that Roffrey didn't really like anyone—apart from his wife. It was a great pity that he'd found her, Mordan reflected.

Selinsky and his assistants pored over their findings. Mann, although a good and clever scientist, was beginning to tire of the routine work. As they paused for coffee, he said to Selinsky:

'Something occurred to me, professor, which may mean nothing, but it's worth throwing out for discussion, I think.'

Selinsky, who disapproved of Mann's weakness for theorising while on the job, said impatiently: 'What is?'

'Well, in the history we got from records, both Talfryn and Roffrey were on that planet they call Roth—in the Sundered Worlds—the "lattice planet." Parts of it exist in different continuua, rather like Asquiol is supposed to do. Could this planet have exerted some kind of influence on them? Or perhaps if they stood the test of staying sane on Roth—it turned Roffrey's wife mad, remember they are therefore better fitted for fighting the aliens?'

Selinsky drained his coffee cup and ran a finger across his wet lips.

'There may be something there,' he said. 'Look, I'll tell you what. Work something out properly, in your spare time, and show me your ideas in a report.'

'Spare time!' Mann said explosively, though he was pleased at Selinsky's encouragement—a rare thing in itself.

'Well, you can't sleep *all* of those six hours,' said Zung quietly, grinning to himself as he went back to his work.

Willow Kovacs felt more resigned now. Roffrey had been away too long for there to be much chance of his coming back soon. She calmly filled the hypo and gave Mary another sedative, but she didn't, after all, take one herself. In this calmer frame of mind her thoughts had again turned to Asquiol. She must contact him, she felt. At least she would have a clearer idea of how to act after she had seen him—whatever happened.

She experienced some difficulty in getting Roffrey's communications equipment to work, but finally she contacted Mordan.

The Gee-lord's sagging face appeared on the screen. He was hunched over his desk apparently doing nothing. He looked incredibly tired. Willow decided he must be keeping himself awake with stimulants.

He gave her a nod of recognition and said: 'Miss Kovacs, if you're worried about Roffrey and Talfryn, there's no need. They have been recruited as Gamblers and will no doubt be getting in touch with you during a rest period.'

'Thanks,' she said, 'but there was something else.'

'How important is it, Miss Kovacs? You understand that I'm very . . .'

'I wish to contact Asquiol directly.'

'That's impossible now. And, anyway, you wouldn't find it desirable if you realised what he looks like. What do you want to say to him?'

'I can't deal through someone else—it's a purely personal matter.'

'Personal? I remember—you had some emotional relationship . . .'

'We were very close on Migaa and on the Shifter worlds. I'm sure he would want to see me.' She didn't sound as if she particularly believed her own words.

'Next time I report to him I'll pass your message on. That's all I can do, I'm afraid.' Mordan stared curiously at her but said nothing more.

'Will he contact me if he gets your message?'

'If he wants to that's exactly what he will do. I'll tell him what you've said—I promise.'

The screen shimmered and was empty again. Willow turned it off and walked slowly back to where Mary was sleeping.

'What's going to happen to you in all this?' she said.

There was in Willow a large capacity for sympathy with those in distress. Even now, with troubles of her own which she hadn't counted on before she'd reached the fleet, she could turn her attention to Mary.

But what had at first been a detached emotion of sympathy such as she could feel towards anyone in an unpleasant predicament, was fast running into a less healthy feeling. She was beginning to sense a kinship with Mary. They were both very lonely women—the one lacking any contact with her fellows, trapped inside her disturbed and jumbled mind, veering between near-sanity and complete madness; the other with a growing conviction that, in her moment of need, she had been deserted—not only by Asquiol, but by Talfryn and Roffrey too.

She sat by the screen, waiting for Asquiol to contact her. She sat stiffly. The cabin was silent, as silent as the space through which the fleet moved. She shared with the rest of humanity a demoralised, disillusioned sense of loss, of unknowing, of confusion. And as in the rest of them, these feelings were crystallising into fear.

Only the certain knowledge that loss of control at this time would bring certain destruction of mind or body allowed them to keep going.

Kept active by drugs, sent to sleep by sedatives, driven by the uncompromising will of Asquiol and his tool Mordan, the Gamblers prepared for another round of the Game.

FIFTEEN

They were seated in threes, each group before a large screen which mirrored the scene on the huge screen over their heads. The large chamber was dark, illuminated solely by light from instruments and screens. Below the small screens were even smaller ones, in two rows of six. Mordan, who had brought Talfryn and Roffrey into the chamber, explained in a soft voice what purpose they served.

Roffrey looked about him.

Three sections of the circular chamber were occupied with the screens and seated before them each had its trio of operators—pale, thin men and women, for the most part, living off nervous energy and drugs. They had glass-alloy caps, similar to those he had worn while taking the tests. No one looked up as he entered.

'The screen above us is, as you can see, merely a wide-angle viewer which enables us to scan the space immediately around the fleet,' Mordan was saying.

'Each group of operators—Gamblers we call them—is delegated a certain area of this space to watch for signs of alien expedition. So far as we can gather, it is part of their code to come close—within firing range—to our fleet before beginning the round. Apart from that, we are given no warning that a fresh round is about to commence. That's why we keep constant watch. Presumably among themselves the aliens have subtler ways of beginning, but this seems to be their compromise.

'When an alien expedition comes into sight, the team sighting it alerts the rest and they all concentrate on that area. The smaller rows of screens record the effect which we beam towards the aliens. They record hallucinatory impulses, and these are broken down into sections governed by the different senses, brain-waves of varying frequencies, emotional-impulses such as fear, anger and so on, which we are capable of simulating. We have, of course, projectors, magnifiers and broadcasting equipment which is capable of responding to the commands of the Gamblers. But primarily, in the last resort, everything depends on the imagination, quick reactions, intelligence and ability to simulate emotions, thoughts and so on, which each individual Gambler possesses.'

'I see.' Roffrey nodded. In spite of himself, he was interested. 'What happens then?'

'Just as many of our emotions and impulses are unfamiliar and incommunicable to the aliens, the same applies to us. Presumably half the impressions and mental impulses we have flung at us do not have the effect the aliens desire, or would get in their own kind. But we have the same difficulty.

'These men have been playing the Game long enough to recognise whether the effects they send are effective or not, and can guard against those effects which are most dangerous to us. Winning the Game, at this stage, anyway, depends largely upon the extent to which we can assimilate and analyse what works and what doesn't work. This also, of course, applies to the aliens. You, for instance, had the hallucination of a monster beast which shocked not only your instincts, triggering fear, panic, and so on, but shocked your logical qualities since you knew that it was impossible for such a beast to exist in the vacuum of space.'

Roffrey and Talfryn agreed.

'This sort of effect is what the aliens are relying on—although in the general run of things these days they have learned to be much more subtle, working directly on the subconscious as they did to a large extent on you, after the beast-image didn't get the result they wanted. Therefore

131

our psychologists and other researchers are gathering together every scrap of information which each round gives us, trying to get a clear picture of what effects will have the most devastating results on the *alien*'s subconscious. Here, as I mentioned, we are fairly well matched—our minds are as alien to them as theirs are to us.

'The prime object in playing the Blood Red Game, therefore, is to find the exact impulse necessary to destroy the qualities which we term self-respect, strength of character, intrinsic confidence, and so on.'

Mordan exhaled heavily.

'The number of losses we've had can be assessed when I tell you that we've got two hundred men and women alone who are curled up into foetal balls in the wards of our hospital ships.'

Talfryn shuddered. 'It sounds revolting.'

'Forget that,' Mordan said curtly. 'You'll lose all sense of moral values after you've been playing the Game for a short time. The aliens are helping us to do what philosophers and mystics have been preaching for centuries. Remember it? *Know thyself*, eh?'

He shook his head, staring grimly around the chamber where the grey-faced Gamblers watched the screens concentratedly.

'You'll get to know yourself here all right. And I'm sure you won't like what you learn.'

'Easier on the brooder, the introvert,' Roffrey said.

'How deep can one man go in probing his innermost impulses before he pulls back—out of self-protection if nothing else?' Mordan said sharply. 'Not far in comparison to what the aliens can do to you. But you'll find out.'

'You're giving an attractive picture,' Roffrey said.

'Damn you, Roffrey—I'll talk to you after your first round. This may, now I come to think of it, do you an awful lot of good!'

They were joined by a third individual. He had obviously been a Gambler for some time. They were beginning to recognise the type. He was tall, thin and nervous.

'Fiodor O'Hara,' he said, not bothering to shake hands. They introduced themselves in the same curt manner.

'You will be in my charge until you become familiar with the Game,' O'Hara said. 'You will obey every order I give you. Try not to resist me. The sooner you are trained, the sooner you will be able to play the Game without any direction. I believe you are what they call an individualist, Roffrey. Well, you will have to conform here until you have mastered the Game—then your individualism will doubtless be of great use, since we depend on such qualities.

'Most of the people here are trained in some branch of psychology, but there are a few like yourselves—laymen—who have a sufficiently high I.Q. to be receptive, almost instinctively, to the needs of the Game. I wish you luck.

'You will find it a great strain to keep your ego free and functional—that is really all you have to learn to do as a beginner. You will carry out defensive strategy, as it were, until you are adept enough to begin attacking the enemy. Remember, both of you, physical strength and daring mean absolutely nothing in this war. And you lose not your life, but your sanity—at first anyway.'

Roffrey scratched the back of his neck.

'For God's sake, let's get started,' he said, impatiently.

'Don't fret,' Mordan said as he left them. 'You'll soon know when another round begins.'

O'Hara took them to a row of empty seats. There were three seats, the usual screen and the miniature screens beneath it. Immediately in front of them were small sets of controls which were evidently used to operate the sense-projectors and other equipment.

'We have a short vocabulary which we shall use later for communication while the Game is in progress,' O'Hara said, settling the skull-cap on his head. 'Switch sound, for instance, means that if, at a certain moment, you are concentrating on taste sensations, I have decided that sounds would be more efficient against the enemy. If I say, "Switch-taste," it means that you send taste-impressions. That is simple—you understand?'

They showed their assent. Then they settled themselves to await their first—and perhaps—last round of the Blood Red Game.

The morality of what they were doing—invading this universe and attempting to wrest dominance of it from the native race—had bothered Asquiol little.

'Rights?' he had said to Mordan when the Gee-lord had relayed the doubts of some of the members of the fleet. 'What rights have they? What rights have we? Because they exist here doesn't mean that they have any special *right* to exist here. Let them, or us, *establish* our rights. Let us see who wins the Game.'

Asquiol had more on his mind than a squabble over property, dangerous as that squabble could be for the race.

This was Man's last chance of attaining his birthright—something which Asquiol had almost attained in his ability to perceive simultaneously the entire universe—to take over from the Originators.

Somehow he had to teach his race to tap its own potential. Here, those Gamblers who might survive would be of use.

The race had to begin on the next stage of its evolution, yet the transition would have to be so relatively sudden that it would be virtually revolution.

And there was the personal matter of his *incompleteness* the torturing frustration of knowing that the missing piece that would make him whole was so close—he could sense it—as to be almost within his grasp. But what was it?

Dwelling in thought, Asquiol was grave.

Even he could not predict the eventual outcome if they won the Game. More able to encompass the scope of events than the rest of the race, in some ways he was as much in a temporal vacuum as they were—quite unable to relate past experience with present, or the present with whatever the future was likely to be.

He existed in all the many dimensions of the multiverse. Yet he was bound by the single multiversal dimension of Time almost as much as anyone else. He had cast off chains of space but was tied, as perhaps all denizens of the multiverse would always be, by the steady-paced, imperturbable prowl of Time, which brooked no halt, which condoned no tampering with its movement, whether to slow it or to speed it.

Time, the changer, could not be changed. Space, perhaps, the material environment, could be conquered. Time, never. It held the secret of the First Cause—a secret not known even to the Originators who had built the great, finite multiverse as a seeding bed—a womb—for their successors. But should the human race survive the birth-pangs and succeed the Originators, Asquiol felt that it would not present a key to the secret.

Perhaps, in many generations—each generation measured as a stage in Man's evolution—it would be found. But would the solution to the puzzle be welcomed? Not by his race—

but maybe its great-grand-children would be capable of accepting and retaining such knowledge. For once they replaced the Originators they would have the task of creating *their* successors. And so it would continue, perhaps *ad infinitum*—to what greater purpose?

He stopped this reverie abruptly. In this respect he was a pragmatist. He could not concern himself with such pointless speculation.

There was a lull in the Game. The coming of Roffrey's ship and its defeat of the aliens had evidently non-plussed them for a while. But Roffrey, so far, had not experienced the real struggle which was between minds, trained minds capable of performing the most savage outrage there could be—destroying the id, the ego, the very qualities that set man above other beasts.

For a moment he wondered about Talfryn, but stopped the train of thoughts since it led to another question troubling him.

Asquiol allowed his concentration to cease for a moment as he enjoyed the rich nourishment that experience of dwelling on all planes of the multiverse gave him. He thought: *I am like a child in a womb, save that I know I am in the womb. Yet I am a child with a part missing, I sense it. What is it? What will complete me? It is as if the part would not only complete me, but complete itself at the same time.*

As was happening increasingly, he was interrupted by a sharp signal from the communicator.

He leaned forward in his chair, the strange shadows and curious half-seen images dancing about his. As he moved, the area of space between him and the communicator seemed to spray apart, flow and move spasmodically like water disturbed by the intrusion of an alien body. This happened whenever he moved, although he himself was only aware of his passing his arm through many objects which exerted a very faint pressure upon his limbs.

He could not only see the multiverse, he could also feel it, smell it, taste it. Yet this was little help in dealing with the aliens, for he found it almost as difficult as the rest of his race to understand the actual psychology of the non-human attackers.

The communicator came to life.

'Yes?' he said.

135

Again, Mordan had not turned on his own receiver, so that whereas Asquiol could see him, he need not subject himself to the eye-straining sight of Asquiol's scintillating body.

'A few messages,' Mordan went through them quickly. 'Hospital ship OP8 has disappeared. We heard that the I.T. field was becoming erratic. They were repairing it when they just . . . faded out of space. Any instructions?'

'I saw that happen. They're safe enough where they are. No instructions. If they're lucky they'll be able to rejoin the fleet if they can adjust their field.'

'Roffrey and Talfryn, the two men who succeeded in withstanding the B.R. effect so successfully, have been subjected to all Professor Selinsky's tests and he is studying the results now. In the meantime they are being taught how to play the Game.'

'What else?' Asquiol observed Mordan's worried expression.

'There were two women on Roffrey's ship. One of them was the mad woman—Mary Roffrey. The other calls herself Willow Kovacs. I have already forwarded this information to you, you remember.'

'Yes. Is that all?'

'Miss Kovacs asked me to pass a message on to you. She says that you were personally acquainted on Migaa and later in the Shifter. She would like it if you could spare the time to get in touch with her. The ship is on 050 L metres for tight contact.'

'Thank you.'

Asquiol switched out and sat back in his seat. There was in him still some part of the strong emotion he had felt for Willow. But he had had to rid himself of it twice. Once when she had declined to follow him to Roth, once after he met the Originators. His impression of her was, by now, a little vague—so much had happened.

He had had to dispense with many valuable emotions when he assumed control of the fleet. This was out of no spirit of ambition or will to dominate. It was simply that his position demanded maximum control of his mind. Therefore emotions had to be sacrificed where they could not directly contribute to what he was doing. He had become, in so far as ordinary human relationships were included, a very lonely man. His perception of the multiverse had more than compensated for the breaks in human contact he had been forced to make, but he rather wished that he had not had to make those breaks.

Normally, he never acted on impulse, yet now he found himself turning his communicator dial to the wavelength 050 L metres. When it was done he waited. He felt almost nervous.

Willow saw her screen leap into life and she quickly adjusted her own controls with the information indicated above the screen. She acted hurriedly, excitedly, and then the sight she saw froze her for a moment.

After that, her movements were slower as she stared fascinatedly at the screen.

'Asquiol?' she said in a faltering voice.

'Hello, Willow.'

The man still bore the familiar facial characteristics of the Asquiol who had once raged through the galaxy spreading chaos and laughter in his wake.

She remembered the insouciant, moody youth she had loved. But this . . . this Satan incarnate sitting in its chair like some fallen archangel—this golden sight bore no relation to him as she remembered him.

'Asquiol?'

'I'm deeply sorry,' he said, and smiled at her with a melancholy look for an archangel to wear.

Her face reflected the peculiar dancing effect which the image on the screen produced. She stepped back from it and stood with her shoulders drooping. And now she had only the memory of love.

'I should have taken my chance,' she said.

'There was only one, I'm afraid. If I'd known, I perhaps could have convinced you to come with us. As it was I didn't want to endanger your life.'

'I understand,' she said. 'Tough for me, eh?'

He didn't reply. Instead he was glancing behind him.

'I'll have to switch out—our opponents are starting another round of the Game. Goodbye, Willow. Perhaps, if we win, you and I can have another talk.'

But she was silent as the golden, brilliant image faded from the screen.

SIXTEEN

O'Hara turned to his companions.

'This is your trial,' he said. 'Get ready.'

There was a faint humming sensation in the huge, circular chamber.

O'Hara had adjusted his screen so that he could now see the alien ships swimming through space towards them. Only a few miles from the fleet they came to a stop and remained, in relation to the fleet, in a fixed position.

Roffrey suddenly found himself thinking of his childhood, his mother, what he had thought of his father and how he had envied his brother. Why should he suddenly decide to . . .? Hastily he pulled himself out of this reverie, feeling slightly nauseated by a random thought that had begun to creep into his conscious mind. This was akin to what he'd experienced earlier, but not so intense.

'Careful, Roffrey—it's beginning,' said O'Hara.

And it was only a mild beginning.

Whatever the aliens had learned of the human subconscious, they used. However, they had gained such a store of information, Roffrey would never know—though the human psychiatrists had a similar store of 'weapons' to turn back against their enemies.

Every dark thought, every unhealthy whim, every loathsome desire that they had ever experienced was dredged up by the alien machines and shoved before their conscious minds.

The trick, as O'Hara had said, was to forget values of good and evil, right and wrong, and to accept these impressions for what they were—desires and thoughts shared by everyone to some degree.

But Roffrey found it hard going.

And this was not all. The alien means of triggering these thoughts was spectacular and mind-smashing in its incredibly clever intensity.

He found it difficult to define between what was sight or smell, taste or sound.

And pervading it all, in the aching background of everything, was the swirling, whirling, chattering, shrieking, odorous, clammy, painful colour—the blood red sense.

It was as if his mind had exploded. As if it were gouting its contents, awash with blood and the agony of naked thoughts, unclothed by prejudice and self-deception. There was no comfort in this world he had suddenly entered—no release, no rest or hope of salvation. The alien sensory-projectors were forcing him further and further into his own mind, jumbling what was there when it did not suit their purpose to show it to him as it really was. All his conscious thoughts and senses were scrambled and jellied and altered. All his subconscious feelings were halted before him and he was forced to look.

In the back of his mind was a small spark of sanity repeating over and over again: 'Keep sane—keep sane—hang on—it doesn't matter—it's all right.' And at times he heard his own voice blended with dozens of others as he howled like a dog and cried like a child.

Yet in spite of all this that was flung against him and the rest, in spite of the loathing he began to feel for himself and his fellows, there was still the spark which kept him sane.

It was at this spark that the aliens aimed their main concentration, just as the more experienced Gamblers in the human ranks aimed to destroy the little sparks of sanity alive in their opponents.

Never in the history of the human race had such dreadful battles been fought. This was more like a war between depraved demons than between material creatures.

It was all Roffrey could do to keep that spark alive as he sweated and struggled against the columns of sound, the vast, booming waves of smells, in the groaning movement of colour.

And as if in keeping with this battleground, the blood red mingling of senses swam and ran and convulsed and heaved themselves through his racked being, hurled themselves along his neural tracts, hacked past his cortical cells, mauled his synapses and shook body and brain into a formless, useless jelly of garbled receptions.

Blood red! There was nothing now save the blood red shrilling of a pervading, icy, stinking taste and a washed-out feeling of absolute self-loathing that crept in everywhere, in every cranny and corner of his mind and person so that he wanted nothing more than to shake it aside, to escape from it.

But it trapped him—the blood red trap from which he could only escape by retreating back down the corridors of his experience, to huddle comfortingly in the womb of . . .

The spark flared and sanity returned completely for a moment. He saw the sweating, concentrated faces of the other operators. He saw Talfryn's face writhing and heard the man groaning, saw O'Hara's thin hand on his shoulder and grunted an acknowledgement. He glanced at the tiny screen which was fluttering with dancing graphs and pulsating light.

Then he was reaching for the small control panel before him, and his bearded face bore a twisted half-smile as he shouted:

Cats!'

'And they crawl along your spines with their claws gripping your nerves.

'Tides of mud, oozing. Drown, creatures, drown!'

The words themselves were of little effect, but they were not meant to be—they were triggering off emotions and impressions in his own mind.

He was attacking now! Using the very emotions and impressions which the aliens had released. And he had grasped some understanding of how they could react to these things, for there had been in their attack several impressions which had meant nothing to him, translated into his own terms. These he flung back with a will and his own screens began to lap to the horrid rhythms of his savagely working mind.

First he sent the blood red impressions back, since these were obviously a preliminary attack which formed the basis of the Game. He didn't understand why this should be, but he was learning quickly. And one of the things he had learned was that reason played little part while the Game was on. That instinct had to be turned into a fighting tool. Later the experts could analyse results.

But then he felt the hysteria leave him and there was silence in the chamber.

'Stop! Roffrey—stop! It's over—they won. Christ! We haven't got a hope now!'

'Won?. I haven't finished . . .'

'Look—'

Several of the Gamblers were sprawled on the floor, mewling and drooling insanely. Others were curled into tight foetal balls. Attendants rushed in to tend to them.

'We've lost seven. That means the aliens won. We got perhaps five. Not bad. You nearly had your opponent, Roffrey, but they've pulled back now. You'll probably get another chance. For a first-timer you did exceptionally well.'

Talfryn was insensible when they turned their attention to him.

O'Hara appeared unconcerned. 'He's lucky—it looks as if he's only blacked out. I think he's tough enough to take another round or two now he's got used to the Game.'

'It was—filthy . . .' Roffrey said. His whole body was tight with strain, his nerves were bunched, his head ached terribly, his heart pumped wildly. He even found it hard to focus on O'Hara.

Seeing his trouble, O'Hara took a hypodermic from a case in his pocket and gave Roffrey an injection before he could protest.

Roffrey began to feel better. He still felt tired, but his body started to relax and the headache was less intense.

'So that's the Blood Red Game,' he said after a moment.

'That's it,' said O'Hara.

Selinsky studied the papers Mann had prepared for him.

'You may well have something here,' he said. 'It is possible that the Shifter exerts a particular influence on the human mind that equips that mind for withstanding the attacks of the aliens.'

'He looked up and spoke to Zung, who was fiddling with some equipment in one corner of the room.

'You say that Roffrey stood up particularly well in his first round?'

'Yes,' the little Mongolian nodded. '*And* he resumed the attack without direction. That's rare.'

'He's valuable enough without having any special characteristics,' Selinsky agreed.

'What do you think of my suggestions?' Mann said, almost impatiently, wanting to get back to his own line of inquiry.

'Interesting,' Selinsky said, 'but still nothing very definite to go on. I think we might ask to see Roffrey and Talfryn and find out what we can about their experiences in the Shifter.'

'Shall I ask them to come here?' Zung suggested.

'Yes, will you?' Selinsky frowned as he studied Mann's notes.

From the turmoil that was her ruined brain, Mary was emerging. Half afraid, for the knowledge of her insanity preyed always on her sane mind, she was reassembling her reason.

Suddenly there was no more confusion. She lay there, eyes seeing nothing at all—no sights of disordered creation, no threatening creatures, no danger. All she heard was the slight scuffling sound of somebody moving about near her.

Very carefully, she thought back.

It was hard to distil a sense of time out of the chaos of memory. It had been as if she had spent most of her life in a whirlpool, performing such meaningless actions as piloting a ship, opening airlocks, making equations on pads that flowed away from her and disappeared.

There had been periods when the turmoil of the whirlpool had abated—sane periods where she had hovered on the brink of insanity but never quite succumbed. There had been the first arrival at the Shifter, looking for the knowledge she had found on Golund. There had been a landing on Entropium, and then a chaotic journey among the planets through space that contained no laws, only a turbulent inconsistency; landing, finding nothing, keeping a hold on her sanity which kept threatening to crack; and finally to Roth where her mind had gone completely. Aware of warmth. Then away from Roth in a manner she could never remember, back to Entropium; a man who asked her questions—Jon Renark—and the horror of half-sanity finally smashed by the cataclysm that had turned Entropium into rubble; the dash for the Hauser, crashing on a peaceful planet—Ekiversh, perhaps?—and resting, resting—then on to Roth . . . chaos . . . warmth . . . chaos . . .

Why?

What had kept pulling her back to Roth, so that every time she returned her sanity had given out a little more, a little more? But the last time there had been something extra—a turning point, as if she had gone full circle, on the road *back* to sanity. She had met entities there, things of

142

formless light that had spoken to her. No, that was probably an hallucination . . .

With a healthy sigh she opened her eyes. Willow Kovacs stood over her. Mary recognised the woman who had comforted her. Mary smiled.

'Where's my husband?' she said quietly, and composed her features.

'Feel better now?' Willow said. The smile she gave in reply was sorrowful, but Mary saw it was not her that Willow pitied.

'Much. Is Adam . . .?'

'He's been recruited to play this Game.' Briefly Willow explained all she knew. 'He should be getting in touch soon.'

Mary nodded. She felt rested, at peace. The horror of her madness was a faint memory which she pushed further and further back. Never again, she thought. That was it—I'm all right now. That was the last time. She felt herself drifting into a deeper, more natural sleep.

Roffrey and Talfryn entered Selinsky's lab. Roffrey, huge and powerful, his black beard seeming to bristle with vitality, said:

'More tests, professor?'

'No captain. We wish merely to question you on one or two points which have cropped up. To tell you the truth, neither of you appears to possess any strong trait which can account for your besting so many opponents. We have discovered that the reason you were able to beat those ships with such apparent ease was that *every* one of their Gamblers was beaten—put out of action by some force so powerful that it crossed space without any sending equipment to aid it. Their receivers turned the emanations into a force which destroyed their minds completely. But you possess no qualities of sufficient strength which could account for this. It is as if you needed an . . . amplifier of some kind. Can you explain that?'

Roffrey shook his head.

But Talfryn was frowning and said nothing. He appeared thoughtful. 'What about Mary?' he said slowly.

'Yes, that may be it!' Zung looked up from his notes.

'No, it isn't,' Roffrey said grimly.

Talfryn broke in: 'She's the one. Your wife, Roffrey. She

143

was absolutely crazy on Éntropium. She travelled between the Shifter's planets when space was wild and chaotic. She must have had a tremendous reserve of control somewhere in her if she could stand what she did. She could have picked up all kinds of strange impressions that worked on her brain. She did, in fact. She's our amplifier!'

'Well, what about it?' Roffrey turned round and looked at the three scientists standing there eagerly, live vultures who had spotted a dying traveller.

Selinsky sighed.

'I think we're right,' he said.

Mary stared out at the hazy light of the fleet dropping through darkness towards the far-off stars gleaming like lights at the end of a long, long tunnel.

'Adam Roffrey,' she said aloud, and wondered what she would feel when she saw him.

'How did you get to the Shifter?' Willow asked from where she sat.

'I ran away from Adam. I got tired of his restless life, his constant hatred of civilisation and ordered society. I even tired of his conversation and his jokes.

'Yet I loved him. Still do. I'm an anthropologist by profession, and took advantage of Adam's trips to the remote outworlds to keep my hand in. One time, we landed on Golund—the planet with signs of having been visited by a race from another galaxy. I hunted around the planet but got no more than the scant information available. So I left Adam and went to the Shifter when it materialised in our space-time, hoping to find some clues there. I searched the Shifter system, I searched it and clung to my sanity by a thread. But Roth was the last straw, Roth finished me.

She turned back to look at Willow, smiling. 'But now I feel saner than I've ever done—and I'm thinking of settling down if I can. Becoming a good little wife to Adam. What do you think of that, Willow?' Her eyes were serious.

'I think you're nuts,' Willow said tactlessly. 'Don't sell out for the easy life. Look at me . . .'

'It's been hard, though,' said Mary, staring at the floor. 'Far too hard, Willow.'

'I know,' she said.

The communicator whistled. Mary went to it, operated the control.

It was Roffrey.

'Hello, Adam,' she said. Her throat felt constricted. She put her hand to it.

'Thank God,' he said, his weary face impassive.

She knew she still loved him. That alone was comforting.

'You got a doctor, then?' he said.

'No,' she said smiling. 'Don't ask me how—just accept that I'm sane. Something happened—the fight with the aliens, something on Roth, maybe just Willow's nursing. I don't know. I feel a new woman.'

His face softened as he relaxed. He grinned at her. 'I can't wait,' he said. 'Can you and Willow come over to the Game Ship right away? That's what I contacted you for—before I knew.'

'Certainly,' she said. 'But why?'

'The people here think that all four of us, as a sort of team, managed to beat off the alien sense-impression attack. They want to give you a few routine tests along with Willow. Okay?'

'Fine,' she said. 'Send over a launch to collect us and we'll be with you.'

She thought she saw him frown just before he switched out.

Much later, Selinsky screwed up his tired face and pushed his hand over it. He shook his head briskly as if to clear it, staring at the two women who, under sedatives, lay asleep in the testing chairs.

'There's certainly something there,' he said, rolling a small light-tube between his palms. 'Why couldn't we have tested all four of you together? A stupid oversight.' He glanced at the chronometer on his right index finger.

'I've no idea why, but Asquiol is to broadcast to the entire fleet in a little while. About the Game, I think. I hope the news is good—we could do with some.'

Roffrey was ill at ease, brooding, paying scant attention to the scientist. He stared down at Mary and he suddenly felt weak, ineffectual, as if he no longer played a part in her life, and could hardly control his own. An unusual feeling—connected, perhaps, with the shape that events seemed to be taking . . .

Now she remembered. As she slept, physically, her mind was alert. She remembered landing on Roth, of stumbling

145

over the surface, of falling down an abyss that took her upwards; of the strange, warm things that had entered her brain . . . She remembered all this because she could sense something similar quite close to her. She reached out to try and contact it, but failed—only just failed. She felt like a climber on a cliff-face who was reaching for the hand of the climber just above, the fingers stretching out carefully, desperately, but not quite touching.

There was somebody out there—somebody like her—but more like than she was. That was the impression she got. Who or what was it? Was it a person, such as she defined the word, or something else?

Adam? No, it wasn't Adam. She realised she had spoken his name aloud.

'I'm here,' he said, smiling down at her. She felt his big hand grasping her firmly, encouragingly.

'Adam . . . there's something . . . I don't know . . .'

Selinsky appeared beside her husband. 'How are you feeling?' he asked.

'Fine, physically. But I'm puzzled.' She sat up in the chair, dangling her legs, trying to touch the floor. 'What did you find out?'

'Quite a bit,' he said. 'And we'll be needing you. Are you willing to take a big risk and help us play the Game?'

Mary wondered why her husband was so quiet.

SEVENTEEN

This time, Asquiol realised, he would have to visit the Game Ship personally, for the time he had feared had come.

The aliens had virtually won the Blood Red Game.

Jewelled, the multiverse spread around him, awash with life, rich with pulsating energy, but it could not compensate for his mood of near-despair. Coupled with the empty ache within him, the ache for the missing piece which seemed so close, it threatened to control him.

He still could not trace the source, but it was there. Something, like him but not so developed, was in touch with him—almost the multiverse. He began to put out feelers of his mind into the multiverse, searching.

But then his conscience made him withdraw from this and concentrate once more on the immediate problem. As had happened on past occasions, he had been in communication with the alien leaders. This time they had found it hard to disguise their jubilation, for the Game had taken firm shape.

They were winning. Even with the setback they had received from Roffrey's ship, their score had mounted enormously.

Asquiol still found it difficult to comprehend their method of scoring, but he trusted them. It was unthinkable for them to cheat.

His way of communicating with them was the way he and Renark had learned from the Originator. It wasn't telepathy. It relied on no exact human sense, but involved the use of waves of energy which only one in complete awareness of the multiverse might sense and harness. It did not involve words, but used pictures and symbols. It had been by analysis of some of these symbols which Asquiol had passed on to them that the psychiatrists had managed to devise 'weapons' for use against the aliens.

Asquiol still had no idea of what the aliens called themselves and did not even have a clear impression of their physical appearance. But their messages were easy enough to interpret and the fact remained that the human race had reached a crisis point.

Only one more round of the Game would decide the issue!

Then, if the human race refused to accept the decision and began open war again, Asquiol knew they were doomed, for their fleet was too depleted to stand any chance at all.

News received recently did not alter this certainty. A number of farmships had broken down, others had been lost completely or been destroyed in their early physical encounters with the aliens. Less than two thousand ships of all kinds remained in the fleet—a vast enough caravan by any ordinary standards, but nearly a quarter of a million ships had originally left the home universe.

It was in a mood bordering on hopelessness that he stretched out a scintillating arm and put his communicator on to a general broadcast wavelength to inform the race of what he had learned. It was rare for him to do this, since direct contact with members of his race was becoming increasingly less attractive. He began:

'Asquiol here. Please listen attentively to my message. I have recently been in contact with our attackers and they have informed me that, as far as they are concerned, the game is virtually won—that they are confident that they will be the victors. This means that our position is very nearly hopeless.

'We have, at most, enough supplies to last us for a month. Unless we make planet-fall on some habitable world soon, you will all be dead.

'The only way in which we can survive is to win, decisively, the last round of the Game. The aliens already have a considerable advantage over us and feel that they can, in the next round, sufficiently increase this to ensure victory. Our Gamblers are weary and we have no more recruits. We have drained our talent as we have drained our resources. Our scientists are still working to devise a new way of beating the aliens, but I must tell you that time is running very short. Those among you not directly involved in playing the Blood Red Game had best make what plans you can, bearing in mind what I have said.

'To the Gamblers and all those attached to the Game Ship I can only ask for greater effort, knowing you have worked at full capacity for many days. Remember what we can win. *Everything!* Remember what we stand to lose. *Everything!'*

Asquiol sat back, his message still unfinished, and as he breathed in the exotic scents of the multiverse, he saw the hull of his ship a stark outline against an over-poweringly beautiful background of space alive; sensed, again, that peculiar feeling of kinship with another entity. Where was it? In this universe—or another?

Then he continued:

'I myself will not be directly affected by the outcome, as many of you have guessed. But this is not to say I am unaffected by my trust—to lead the race to safety in the first instance, and to something more in the second. There are those among you who ask what became of my companion Renark, our original leader. You wonder why he stayed behind in the contracting universe. My answer is vague, for neither of us got a clear idea from the Originators why this had to be. It is probably that the stuff of his great spirit was spread amongst us, to give all of us extra vitality—the vitality that we need. It may also have been that he sensed his role finished and mine only to have begun. Perhaps that is an arrogant thing to say.

'Renark was a brave man and a visionary. He was confident that mankind, by its efforts, could avoid, destroy or survive all danger. He was a believer in human Will conquering all obstacles—physical, intellectual, and metaphysical. In this, perhaps, he was naïve. But without that idealism and naïveté, our race could not have survived.

'However, what saved us from one form of peril may not be able to save us from another. Different problems require different solutions. Will alone is not now sufficient to win the Blood Red Game. It must be remembered that the circumstances applying to us in our present predicament are much more complex than they were when Renark and I went on our quest.

'We must be totally ruthless, now. We must be strong and courageous. But we must also be devious, cautious and sacrifice any idealism which made us embark on this voyage. Sacrifice is for survival—and the survival of a greater ideal.'

Asquiol wondered whether to continue. But he decided he had said sufficient for the moment.

Again he sat back, allowing himself to experience full unity with the multiverse.

'*Where are you . . .?*' he said, half-aloud. '*Who are you?*' The need was tangible in him—disconcerting, distracting his attention from the matter he must give all his mind to.

He had already been in contact with the Game Ship and now waited impatiently for the signal which would tell him a vessel was ready to take him there.

He rose and paced the cluttered cabin, the light shivering and breaking apart into rays of shining blue, gold and silver; shadows quivered around him and at times there seemed to be several ghostly Asquiols in the cabin.

At length the launch clamped against the side of his ship and he passed through his airlock and into the cramped cabin of the launch. Quickly it cruised over to the Game Ship and eased sideways into a receiving bay. The great outer doors closed down swiftly and Asquiol stepped out to be greeted by Lord Mordan.

'Perhaps,' he said, 'with your aid, Asquiol . . .'

But Asquiol shook his iridescent head. 'I have little special power,' he said. 'I can only hope that my aid will help the Gamblers to hang on a little longer.'

'There is something else. Selinsky wants to see you. It appears that all four of those people who came in from the Shifter have some kind of group-power . . .'

They were striding along the corridors, their boots clanging on metal.

Asquiol said, 'I'll speak to Selinsky now.'

He stopped as Mordan paused beside a door. 'This is Selinsky's lab.'

'Is he in?'

Mordan turned a stud and entered. Selinsky looked up, blinking as Asquiol followed Mordan in.

'An honour . . .' he said, half-cynically.

'Lord Mordan tells me, professor, that you are on to some new development?'

'Yes, that's so. The woman—Mary Roffrey. She's not only sane now, she's . . . what? Super-sane! Something was done to her mind on Roth. The whole nature of it altered. It is very different from anyone else's—except, perhaps . . .'

'Mine?' Asquiol felt excitement creeping through him. 'Is she, then, like me—as you see me?'

Selinsky shook his head. 'She seems perfectly normal—until you analyse her brain structure. She's what we need, all right.'

Asquiol was beginning to see the pattern now. Was this woman the missing piece in his existence? Had the Originators done something to her brain in order to form her into what she potentially was—a weapon? He could only guess.

Selinsky said: 'She wasn't a product of the alien attack at all. She was a product of more than just a series of madness-inducing hallucinations on Roth. Something or somebody had actually tampered with her brain. It's the most delicately balanced thing I've ever seen!'

'What do you mean?' Asquiol asked.

'One way—utter madness; the other way—unguessable sanity.' Selinsky frowned. 'I'd hate to be in her position. We've got her doing a quick training course with O'Hara at the moment. But playing the Game could ruin her mind for good, tip the balance once and for all.'

'You mean she'd be completely insane?'

'Yes.'

Asquiol pondered. 'We must use her,' he said finally. 'Too much is at stake.'

'Her husband is against the idea, but she seems to be taking it all right.'

'He's the trouble-maker—Roffrey,' Mordan interposed.

'Will he give trouble in this business?'

'He seems resigned,' Selinsky said. 'A strange mood for him. Playing the Game seems to have wrought a change in him. Not surprising . . .'

'I must see her,' Asquiol said with finality, turning to leave the laboratory.

They began the long walk down the corridor to the Game Chamber.

Now Asquiol wanted to see Mary Roffrey—wanted to see her desperately. As he strode along, his mind worked quickly.

Ever since he and Renark had gone to the Shifter, their paths had crossed indirectly. He had never met her—yet she had been the person to supply Renark with a lot of important information without which they might never have reached the Originators. What was she? Some puppet of the Originators which they were using to aid the race? Or was she something more than a puppet?

She must be the missing factor in his own existence. Yet obviously she had no direct contact with the multiverse. She had the power to strike devastatingly back at the aliens—and he had no comparable power. There were things that linked them, yet there were qualities that separated them also. It was as if they both represented certain abilities which Man was capable of possessing. She had something *he* didn't have—he had something *she* didn't have. How similar were they?

This, perhaps, he would find out in a moment.

He went over in his mind the information he had. Mary's mind had been primarily responsible for disorientating the aliens in a wild round of the Game. At that stage she had acted as a conductor for the rest. All of them having been on Roth, they were probably that much more capable of fighting the aliens than anyone else in the fleet. Therefore they would use the other three as well as Mary.

But uppermost in his mind was what Selinsky had just told him.

Mary's mind could improve—or snap irreparably under the stress of this last round.

He knew what he would have to do now. But it was a heavy weight. As he contemplated it, the light around him seemed to fade, become colder and less frenetic in its movement. Sadness, such as he had never thought to experience again, filled him, and he fought it unsuccessfully.

He might, in essence, have to murder a woman—and cut himself off from the power she possessed. The power that was part of him as well as of her.

It was getting late—too late for anything but immediate action. The time of the last round was approaching.

They reached the door of the Game Chamber . . .

EIGHTEEN

In the main chamber, Mary was seated between Willow and listening to the man's briefing. Around them, the other Gamblers were readying themselves for the last round. They looked ill at ease and weary. Many of them did not look up even when Asquiol came in, flinging the door of the chamber open and striding quickly across the great room. The light flowed about the many facets of his body and streamed away behind him. Mary turned round and saw him.

'You!' she said.

A look of puzzlement crossed Asquiol's face. 'We've met?' he said. 'I don't remember.'

'I saw you with Renark several times—on Roth.'

'But we left Roth ages ago!'

'I know—but Roth is a strange planet. Time is non-existent there. Anyway, it wasn't only that.'

'Then how else did you recognise me?'

'I've sensed you've been here all the time. Even before we reached the fleet, I think.'

'But obviously you do not exist, as I do, in the entire multiverse. What could the link be, I wonder?' Then he smiled. 'Perhaps our mutual friends the Originators could tell us.'

'Probably it's simpler than that,' Mary replied. The sense of empathy with Asquiol was like nothing she had ever experienced before. 'Because we have seen them and gained from the contact, we recognise it in each other.'

'Very likely.' He nodded, then suddenly noticed that Willow was staring at him, her eyes full of tears. He took control of himself and said briskly: 'Well, we had better get ready. I'm going to be in control of this project. You, Mary, will work under my direction using—as power, as it were—the other three, Roffrey, Talfryn and Willow. It's quite simple—a sort of gestalt link.'

She looked at the others, who had crossed the room from where Selinsky and his team were working on a mechanism. 'Did you hear that?' Adam had the look of a dumb beast in pain as he stared at her for a moment before dropping his eyes.

'We heard it,' he said. 'All of it.'

She glanced at Asquiol as if seeking his advice, but he couldn't help her. Both of them were now in a similar position—Mary with Roffrey and Asquiol with Willow.

The time was nearing, Mary felt, when she would have to sever her ties with her husband.

The time had passed, Asquiol reflected, when he and Willow could have been united by the common bond which he and Mary possessed.

As they looked at one another, they seemed to convey this without need of speech.

O'Hara interrupted them:

'Get ready, everyone! Remember, we need an over-whelming win in the round that is to follow. This round will be the last we have to play. Winning it must be decisive!'

The five people, Asquiol and Mary in the lead, went towards the specially prepared panel.

Selinsky and his team finished their work and stepped aside.

The five composed themselves to play.

Both Willow and Adam Roffrey had to force themselves to concentrate, but both were motivated by a different fear. Willow feared that Mary would become extra-sane through her ordeal. Roffrey feared she would become insane, while he hated the alternative which would break their relationship before it ever had a chance to resume.

Asquiol was his rival now, Roffrey saw. Yet Asquiol hardly knew it himself.

153

Only Talfryn was not afraid of the possible results. Either way, he felt, he stood to win—so long as Mary was effective in helping the Gamblers win the Game.

Asquiol bent close to Mary and whispered: 'Remember I am in the closest possible touch with you, and you with me. However near you feel you are coming to insanity, don't panic. I'll keep you on the right course.'

She smiled at him. 'Thanks.'

The tension rose as they waited.

It was so delicate, the first probe. As delicate as a slicing scalpel.

O'Hara shouted: 'Don't wait for them. Attack! Attack!'

In contact with Mary now, Asquiol began to dredge up Mary's memories from the deepest recesses of her sub-conscious, doing to her what only a totally evil man might do.

Yet, even as she slipped into the giddy, sickening whirl-pool of insanity, it was obvious to her that Asquiol was not evil. There was no malice in him at all. It was taking fantastic control for him to force himself to continue. But he did continue. He worked at her mind, slashing at it, tearing at it, working it apart in order to remould it, and he did it in the full knowledge that he might, in the final analysis, be committing a dreadful crime.

Beside him, the trio sweated, feeding power to Mary that was channelled by Asquiol and directed by him at the alien attackers.

'There they are, Mary—you see them!'

Mary turned glazed eyes towards the screen.

Yes, she saw them.

It was suddenly like horrible darkness then rolling through her. Red-hot needles forced themselves into the grey mass of her brain. It was like being tightened like a banjo string, together and tighter until she must surely snap. She couldn't ... She couldn't ...

She laughed. It was a huge joke against her. They were all laughing at her.

She sobbed and mewled and lashed back at the pouring stream of demons and hobgoblins that came prancing and tumbling down the long corridors of her mind. They snig-gered and simpered and fingered her brains and her body and pulled her nerves about, enjoying their sport, caressing the parts of her they captured.

She lashed back as the whole scene became pervaded with the blood red sense that had always been there. She knew it. She was familiar with it and she hated it more than anything else.

Gone were emotions—gone self-pity—gone love—gone yearning and jealousy and impotent sadness. The trio linked and locked and lent their strength to Mary. Everything that she felt, they felt. Everything she saw and did, they saw and did. And at times, also, so close were the five blended, they saw something of what Asquiol saw and it lent them strength to pass on to Mary.

On and on they went, driving at the aliens, hating them and sending back impression after impression from the multiple brain.

To the alien players of the Game, it was as if they had suddenly been attacked by an atomic cannon in a war that had previously been fought with swords. They reeled beneath the weight of the attack. They reeled, they marvelled and, in their strange way, they admired. But they fought back even harder, playing, after the initial shock, coolly and efficiently.

Roffrey broke contact at the sound of a voice outside. It was O'Hara shouting: 'We're winning; they were right. Somehow she has the key to the whole mastery of the Game. She does something with her mind that sends exactly the thing most loathsome to them back to them. There's a twist there somewhere that no human experience could have made. She's doing it!'

Roffrey stared at him for a moment as if in panic, and then returned his attention to the Game. For a moment, O'Hara watched him before he returned his own attention. Their gains were slowly mounting—and Mary's inspiration seemed to be encouraging the rest of the Gamblers to give their best.

'This is our finest hour,' O'Hara said thickly. 'Our finest hour.'

And as he passed her he saw Mary's twisted and distorted face with the sweat and saliva all over it, wreathed in the same flickering images that surrounded Asquiol's intent face.

Now she knew she was winning. *Now* she could see they were reeling back. *Now* she felt victory within her reach.

Although the madness was frenzied and all-consuming, there was behind it all the confidence that Asquiol's presence gave her, and she kept sending, though her mind and body ached with searing agony.

Then, quite suddenly, she blacked out, hearing a voice call from a long way off:

'Mary! Mary!'

Asquiol, knowing that he had aided her to reach this state, could hardly bear to continue. But he had to. He put a hand to her sweat-wet hair and dragged the head back to stare into the vacant eyes.

'Mary—you *can* send them away, You *can!*' He began to communicate with her. He forced her attention to the screens.

She threshed in her chair. For a second she stared at him. To his relief he saw sanity there.

'Asquiol,' she said, *'what is it we were?'*

'We can be the same, Mary—now!'

And then she was bellowing in his face, her laughter seeming a physical weight battering around his head so that he wanted to fling up his hands to ward it off, to run and escape, to hide from what he had created. But again he forced control on himself and pushed her face towards the screens.

Roffrey, pain-drunk, glared at him, but did nothing.

Finally, she was roaring and tearing. Asquiol couldn't make contact with her. One of her hands flailed out, the nails slashing his face. Roffrey saw the blood come and was half-astonished. He had forgotten that Asquiol was in many ways as mortal as himself. Somehow it made the feelings in him worse.

Asquiol fought to control this rage, turn it against the aliens. He battled to resume empathetic contact with Mary.

She stirred, her name formed and curled and buzzed through the darkness. She reached out for it.

Elsewhere, many of the Gamblers had already succumbed to the force of the alien impressions. Tidal waves of garbled sense-impressions were being flung against them and even the strongest were finding it hard to resist, to keep the spark of sanity alive and to retaliate.

Asquiol used the communicating-sense that allowed him to contact the aliens and 'converse' with them. He did this to Mary. He shoved impressions and pictures into her mind,

156

things taken from his own memory. And so real did they become, in such close empathy was he with the woman, that he felt his own sanity slipping away. But he was the controlling part of the team—he had to keep aware. He held on for as long as he could, then straightened his back, gasping.

Those watching saw the light surrounding him skip erratically and dim suddenly. Then it became brighter, like a flaring explosion.

And then the light appeared to make contact with Mary. The same thing appeared to happen to her body. Her image split and became many images. . .

Asquiol! ASQUIOL! ASQUIOL!

Hello, Mary.

What is it?

Rebirth. You're whole now.

Is it over?

By no means!

Where are we, Asquiol?

On the Ship.

But it's . . .

Different, I know. Look!

She saw, through facet after facet, her husband, the girl and the other man. They were staring at her in astonishment. Angled, opaque images surrounded every space they did not occupy.

'Adam,' she said, 'I'm sorry.'

'It's all right, Mary. I'm not. Good luck—like I said.' Roffrey was actually smiling.

A new image swam into focus—O'Hara gesticulating.

'I don't know what's happened to the woman and I don't care. Get your attention back to the Game, or it's lost!'

She turned, and the horrifying impressions came back, but it was as if they were pressed through a filter which took away their effect on her mind.

Carefully, she searched her being. She felt Asquiol beside her, felt the warmth of his encouragement. She lashed back, with deliberate and savage fury, searching out weaknesses, using them, splitting the alien minds to shreds. Asquiol guided her—she could feel it. Talfryn, Willow and Adam supplied power and extra impressions which she took and warped and sent out.

More of the Gamblers were dropping out and attendants

were kept busy clearing them from the chamber. There were only five complete teams left.

But it was victory. Mary and Asquiol could feel it as they worked together—oblivious of everything else—to defeat the aliens. They felt at that moment as if they knew everything about their opponents, to such an extent that they were even in danger of giving up out of sympathy.

They fought on, riding a tide of conquest. Soon the entire alien complement was finished. They retreated back and stared around them.

'Asquiol—what happened?'

Asquiol and Mary saw Willow looking up at them. They smiled at her and said:

'This was the Originators' plan, Willow. They obviously did not allow sufficiently for human weakness—but they did not count on the strength of the human spirit, perhaps. Please don't suffer, Willow. You have done more today for humanity than you could ever have done for any single person.'

They turned to regard the others.

'You too, Roffrey—and you, Talfryn. Without you it is unlikely that we could have defeated the alien intelligences. Everything has suddenly become a clear pattern. There was, perhaps, a purpose for Willow and Talfryn when they stayed behind. There was a purpose, also, for Roffrey when he took it into his head to visit the Shifter. We nearly threw away our chance.

'What exactly has happened?' Lord Mordan interrupted. 'Have you become one entity or what?'

'No.' Asquiol spoke with a slight effort. 'It is simply that, existing on the multiversal level, we are capable of linking minds to form a more powerful single unity. That was how we finally defeated our opponents.

'Obviously this was part of the Originators' plan. But they never do anything for us directly. At best, they merely put certain aids in our path. If we can make use of them— assuming we realise what they are—so much to the good. If we can't, we suffer. We were near complete defeat there. If we had not got some hint of Mary's abilities when we did, the plan would have come to nothing. As it was, we were lucky.'

Mary said: 'I must have been watched by the Originators right from the start—even before I met you.'

158

Asquiol continued: 'The Originators make things especially difficult for people they think are . . . material for the new, multiversal race. Simply, only the fittest survive.'

Lord Mordan said obsequiously, yet hastily: 'But the aliens. Can we not discover what our peace terms are? We must hurry . . . the farm-ships . . .'

'Of course,' Asquiol nodded. 'Mary and I will return to my ship and contact them from there.'

Mary and Asquiol moved towards the exit, gave one last glance at the three others, and left.

'What the hell have you got to smile about, Roffrey?' Talfryn said accusingly.

Roffrey felt at peace. Maybe it was the mood induced by weariness, but he didn't think so. There was no more pain in him, no more jealousy, no more hatred. He moved over to the big blank screen and stared up at it. The place suddenly brightened as assistants switched on the central lights and began clearing up the mess the Gamblers had left . . .

'I give up.' Talfryn shook his head, perplexed.

'That's the trouble,' Willow said. 'So many of us do, don't we?'

EPILOGUE

Asquiol of Pompeii took Mary the Maze back to his ship. They felt more at ease there, since the ship bore similarities to their own metabolic state.

Here, with Asquiol acting again as a guide for Mary, they pooled their resources together and contemplated the radiant multiverse around them.

Then they put out a tendril of multiversal thought-matter along the familiar layers, seeking the alien minds.

Then they were in contact!

When the alien leaders came to the ship, Mary gasped and said in normal speech: 'God! They're beautiful.'

They were beautiful, with delicate bones and translucent skins, great, golden eyes and graceful movements. Yet there was a look of depravity about them, of ultimate decadence. Like depraved, wise children.

'The Originators warned me to beware of races they called pessimists,' Asquiol said, 'races who had despaired of ever attaining full awareness of the multiverse, who had so completely lost the urge to transcend their limitations that the tiny core of *being* had, over millennia, been almost completely eroded. Doubtless these are of that kind.'

By use of their unique method, they once again conversed with the aliens and were astonished by the mood of total defeat, unquestioning acceptance of the winners' rights to dictate any terms they wished.

They had lost their urge to transcend physical confines and in so doing had lost pride—real pride, also.

Absolute defeat—lost spirit—utter hopelessness—concede all rights you wish to take . . .

This mood was sufficient to add almost the last pressure on the victors' already weary minds. A great pity welled up in them as they communicated their terms to the conquered.

Accept terms—any terms acceptable—we have no status —you have all status—we are nothing but your tools to use . . .

So conditioned were the aliens to the code applying to the Game they had played for centuries, perhaps millennia, that they could let this unknown opponent do as it liked. They were conditioned to obeying the victor. They could not question the victor's right. Their shame was so intense that they threatened to die of it—yet there was no trace of bitterness, no trace of resentment or lingering pride . . .

Asquiol and Mary resolved to help them, if they could. The aliens left.

Would they ever see them again? As the spherical ship moved away, they sent out a polite impression that congratulated them on their ingenuity and courage, but it met with no response. They were beaten—no praise could alter that. They gave them positions of planets suitable for human occupation—they were totally unsuited for themselves, anyway—and then they fled.

They did not go to nurse grudges, for they had none. They did not plot retaliation, for such a thing was inconceivable. They went to hide—to reappear only if their conquerors demanded it.

They were a strange people whose artificial code had obviously completely superseded natural instincts.

As the alien ship disappeared, Asquiol and Mary broke their contact with the leaders.

'I'd better inform Mordan. He'll be delighted, anyway.' Asquiol operated the laser. He told the Gee-lord of his meeting.

'I'll start the fleet moving towards some habitable planets right away. Give me an hour.' Lord Mordan smiled tiredly. 'We did it, Prince Asquiol. I must admit I was close to accepting defeat.'

'We all were,' Asquiol smiled. 'How are the other three?'

'They've gone back to Roffrey's ship. I think they're okay. Roffrey and the girl seem quite happy, strangely. Do you want me to keep tabs on them?'

'No.' Asquiol shook his head, and as he did so the light broke and reformed around it, the images scattering and merging. Asquiol stared at Mordan's weary face for a moment. The Gee-lord shifted uncomfortably beneath the fixed stare.

'I could do with some natural sleep,' he said at last, 'but I've got to get the fleet moving first. Is there anything else?'

'Nothing,' said Asquiol, and switched out.

There was a subdued mood of victory about the reformed fleet as he and Mary watched it from one of the ports.

'There's a lot more to do, Mary,' he said. 'This is really only the beginning. I once compared the human race to a chick smashing out of its shell. The comparison still applies. We've broken the shell. We've survived our first period in the multiverse—but will we survive the second and the third? Is there a huge, cosmic farmer with an axe somewhere thinking of serving us up for dinner when we're plump enough?'

She smiled. 'You're worn out. So am I. Give yourself time to think properly. It's the reaction—you're depressed. That kind of emotion can harm a lot of the work we still have to do.'

He looked at her in surprise. He was still unused to having company that he could appreciate, someone who could understand what he felt and saw.

'Where are we going?' he said. 'We need to plan carefully. The degraded condition of the fleet can't be allowed to continue once we make planet-fall. Galactic Law will have to be firmly re-established. Men like Lord Mordan, who have been more than useful in the past because of their pragmatic virtues which could not have been helped by possession of the kind of vision we need now, will have to be taken out of positions of power. We've become a grim race lately—out of necessity. If we let matters slide, Mary, the race could easily degenerate back into something worse than its pre-exodus state. If that happened, our destiny might be out of reach for good. There isn't much time. The Originators made that clear when Renark and I first met them.'

He sighed.

'With me to help you,' she said, 'the hard work will be easier. I know it's going to be harder, but there are two of us now. You noticed how Adam and Willow were beginning to respond back in the Game Ship? There must be dozens like them in the fleet, potentially capable of joining us. Soon, perhaps in only a few generations, there will be a race of people like us, until there are enough to take the place of the Originators.'

'Not that many,' Asquiol said. 'Most people are happy as they are. Who can blame them? It will be an uphill climb.'

'That's the best way to climb hills,' she smiled. 'And remember—keep your impression of those aliens we saw firmly in your mind. We have an example now of how we could degenerate. Perhaps it was fated that we should meet that race. It will serve as a reminder—and a warning. And with a reminder like that, we are not likely to fail.'

Around them, as they sat in contemplation, the multi-verse flowed, thick and solid, so full. And this could be the heritage of their race.

He laughed slightly. 'There's a scene in *Henry the Fourth* where Falstaff learns that Prince Hal, his old drinking companion, is now king. He gathers his friends about him and tells them good times have come, for he is "Fortune's Steward," and the king will honour them and allow them to behave as they like with impunity. But, instead, King Henry banishes Falstaff for a buffoon and trouble-maker. Falstaff realises then that instead of becoming better, things are going to be worse. I sometimes wonder if, perhaps, I'm not "Fortune's Steward"—leading the whole race towards a promise I can't keep . . .'

Mary's multi-faceted face smiled encouragingly.

'There are still the Originators. But even without them

Man has always had to act without being able to foresee the outcome of his actions—ever since he began the long climb upward. He is a stumbler; he has to convince himself of the results he will achieve without ever knowing if he can do it. But he quite often succeeds. We have a long way to go, Asquiol, before we shall ever be able to know for certain the outcome of our actions. Meanwhile, we keep going.

'We're probably the most optimistic race in the multiverse!'

They laughed together. And the spirit of Renark, which had permeated through the race to give it a unified strength, seemed to share their joy.

The multiverse, agitated, swirled and leapt and delighted them with its flourish of colour and variety. All possibilities existed there.

All promise, all hope.

Science Fantasy

The Mercurial Mind of
Michael Moorcock

Escape from present-day insanity to new,
different, timeless worlds with Britain's most
imaginative, most original talent. The
following titles are all available in Mayflower:

THE MORNING OF THE MAGICIANS   50p

Louis Pauwels and Jacques Bergier

"Two theories were current in Nazi Germany:
the theory of the *frozen world*, and the theory
of the *hollow Earth*.
"These constitute two explanations of the
world and humanity which link up with
tradition: they even affected some of
Hitler's military decisions, influenced the
course of the war and doubtless contributed
to the final catastrophe. It was through his
enslavement to these theories, and especially
the notion of the sacrificial deluge, that
Hitler wished to condemn the entire German
race to annihilation."

The incredible yet highly regarded theories of
the frozen world and the hollow Earth have
never before been expounded in this country.
They are two amongst many such theories,
including for example man's evolution
towards some kind of mutant superman,
that have remained secret and hidden in
Britain while gaining strong popular support
elsewhere. Now a new awareness is growing
in our minds, and much of our new
understanding we owe to this famous book
and its two intrepid authors. Their
interpretation of human affairs, very
different from that put forward by ordinary
historians and commentators on day-to-day
events, is much nearer to the unexpressed
instincts of the people.

THOSE ABOUT TO DIE   30p
Daniel P. Mannix

"He started forward toward the melee, blood from his wounded side filling up the footprints made by his right foot as he staggered on. The armed *venator* and the spearman exchanged looks. The crowd was shouting, 'No Carpophorus, no!' But Carpophorus paid no attention to them. He was going to get another tiger or die trying."

This infamous but completely factual book tells the story of the Roman Games, where two armies of 5,000 men fought to the death in a show lit at night by human torches. It was the costliest, cruellest spectacle of all time. And hundreds of thousands still crave to satisfy their curiosity about the sport every year – *Those About to Die* is a constantly reprinting bestseller. No other title gives the full facts and paints such a realistic scene: this is an all-the-way book about man's greatest aberration.

KING OIL   30p
Max Catto

The voice of my beloved! he cometh,
Leaping upon the mountains, skipping upon
*   the hills.*   SONG OF SOLOMON

Frank Dibbler, already a millionaire who
wants to be an oil king and become founder
of a dynasty that will perpetuate his name in
the future industrial America that he
foresees, chooses as his wife the daughter of a
Spanish grandee, taking her on the long
hazardous journey from the genteel pomp of
Seville to the vast, untamed ranch-land of
Texas.

This epic yarn is Max Catto's finest and most
gripping novel.